The Dangerous Age

The Dangerous Age

LETTERS AND FRAGMENTS FROM A WOMAN'S DIARY

Karin Michaëlis

With a Foreword by Phyllis Lassner

NORTHWESTERN UNIVERSITY PRESS
EVANSTON, ILLINOIS

Northwestern University Press
Evanston, Illinois 60201

Originally published in Danish as *Den farlige alder; breve og dagbogsoptegnelser* by Gyldendal, Copenhagen, 1910. *The Dangerous Age* first published 1911 by John Lane Company. Foreword copyright © 1991 by Northwestern University Press. This edition published 1991. All rights reserved.

Printed in the United States of America

ISBN: 0-8101-1015-6 (cloth)
0-8101-1040-7 (paper)

Library of Congress Cataloging-in-Publication Data

Michaëlis, Karin, 1872–1950.
The dangerous age : letters and fragments from a woman's diary / Karin Michaëlis ; with a foreword by Phyllis Lassner.
p. cm.
Originally published: New York : J. Lane Co., 1911.
ISBN 0-8101-1015-6 (alk.paper : cloth). – ISBN 0-8101-1040-7 (alk. paper : paper)
I. Title.
PT8175.M5D36 1991
839.8′1372–dc20   91-36148
                                                                      CIP

The paper used in this publication meets the minimum requirements of American National Standard for Information Sciences—Permanence of Paper for Printed Library Materials, ANSI Z39.48-1984.

CONTENTS

Foreword

By Phyllis Lassner

When *The Dangerous Age* was first published in Denmark in 1910 and subsequently translated into twelve languages, it shocked readers for reasons that remain powerful today. Its concern with the "true natures" of women made Karin Michaëlis a media star in her time, responding to calls to defend her views in lectures and magazine and newspaper interviews in Europe and the United States. At a time when science was declaring its own discoveries about women's nature, reviewers such as George Middleton in *The Bookman* (October 1911, 181) were startled by Michaëlis's "moving picture of a woman's emotions over strange hidden places."

The novel appeared at a time ripe for controversy about woman's character and fate. The feminist movement's call for equal rights and choices clashed with the claim, made both by medical scientists and by Freud and other psychologists, that woman's anatomy was her destiny. Human nature may have changed in 1910, as Virginia Woolf proclaimed, but the new psychosexual models simply fixed women's nature in new ways. Because these psychological theories stressed the formative stages of life, marriage and motherhood were still considered the most important aspects of women's lives. In the literature of the period the tri-

1

umphs and failures of courtship, marriage, and motherhood remained the prevailing subjects of female
characterization. Although the New Woman novels of
George Edgerton and Olive Schreiner at the turn of the
century can be seen as challenging the marriage plot and
its idealized "pure woman," their heroines have also
been interpreted as fearful of sex. From Edith Wharton's *The House of Mirth* (1905) to E. M. Forster's
Howards End (1910), heroines succumbed to marriage as
the only pathway to identity and growth, and when that
failed, as with Wharton's Lily Bart, life was over. Even
in suffragist protest literature such as Elizabeth Robins's
Votes for Women (1907), the struggle for women's destiny
is fought as a lovers' quarrel. These works protest
against woman's sexual oppression, yet they limit her
sexuality to the story only of her youth. Thus, in contrast to the literature of its own time, *The Dangerous Age*
is remarkable in exposing prevailing narratives of female
sexual identity as oppressive to women.

     The Dangerous Age remains striking to us because
of the voice of forty-three-year-old Elsie Lindtner.
From the first page of her letters and diaries to the last,
she challenges herself and her readers unrelentingly,
without intervention by any other narrator, about the
politics of women's aging. As she veers from one ex-
treme mood to another, from anger at her women
friends' destructive strategies to desperate loneliness
and remorse and then to empathy with the plights of
other women, Elsie creates a new kind of woman's narrative. The unfolding drama of her midlife crisis becomes a woman's own story of the imprisoning scenarios
of her development.

FOREWORD

Although *The Dangerous Age* sold over one million copies, had three movie versions, and was followed by an almost equally successful sequel, *Elsie Lindtner*, it eventually disappeared from view. Michaëlis's novel was clearly the inspiration for Rose Macaulay's *Dangerous Ages*, published in 1921, but the Danish writer is not known today except for her Bibi books for young people. This outcome coincided with, and may reflect, the loss of interest in women's midlife development that occurred in both scientific and literary inquiries of the time. Only recently, since feminist scholars have restored such texts as Kate Chopin's *The Awakening*, have the experiences of women beyond courtship, marriage, and motherhood begun to be valued.

*   *   *

Karin Michaëlis was born Katharina Brondum in 1872 in the Danish provincial town of Randers. The record of her early years in her memoir, *Little Troll*, reads like a Dickensian scene:

> The little Danish town of Randers is as full of
> crooked lanes and twisted streets as old cream
> is of wrinkles. I was born in this town of half-
> timbered houses and enormous back yards
> during the wildest blizzard of a stormy winter.
> The snow was so deep that four strong men
> had to shovel a path to our house for Mistress
> Fog, the midwife, although we lived in the
> heart of the town, in one of the last houses on
> Poverty Street.

FOREWORD

Like so many of Dickens's characters, Michaëlis's adult views were shaped by her childhood perceptions of family life and its privations. She remembered her mother as the family's sustaining figure. When she was not taking care of her five children or her husband, whose tuberculosis thwarted his career as a civil servant, Mrs. Brondum made wreaths to pay the bills. Michaëlis later paid tribute to her mother in several works from which the oppression of domestic responsibility is seen from the perspective of a child.

Michaëlis's childhood was marked by the affliction of "crossed eyes" which, although surgically corrected, left her with a permanent squint and the fear that she was ugly. This fear was most likely a motivating factor in her adolescent definition of herself as driven by a romantic imagination. Looking back with pain and bemusement, Michaëlis portrays her younger self as proving her sexual attractiveness through the seductive power of her desires. In the summer of her fifteenth year she became secretly engaged to two men, one of whom was scarred like herself; his Byron-like limp seems to have been his main attraction, while the other man seems to have been important only as the object of her adolescent sexuality. At the same time, however, she could not help being affected by the very conservative and pragmatic Danish society in which she lived. A lecture on the necessity for chastity before marriage delivered by the influential Norwegian poet and Nobel laureate Bjornstjerne Bjornson gave the citizens of Randers poetic license to indulge their puritan sensitivities. In this climate it is no wonder that the Brondums were aghast to learn of Katharina's secret loves, which established for them beyond all doubt that their daughter was frivolous and a threat to the family name.

But Michaëlis's youthful romanticism also reflected certain contradictory aspects of Bjornson's ideas. Despite his Calvinist morality, Bjornson glorified Norway's pagan past; and although an unregenerate chauvinist, he nevertheless founded the Norwegian Women's Liberation movement. The Bibi figure of Michaëlis's children's books, like Gunhild in her fictional memoirs, *The Tree of Good and Evil* (1924–39), rebels against traditional definitions of the "good girl." Truants from school and home, both girls tramp the Danish railways and roads in search of self-definition. Michaëlis herself left home, in "voluntary exile," to become a governess to the daughter of a Danish consul on a barren island (*Little Troll*, 64). Under the influence of her own romantic imagination, she dreamed of rescuing her employer from his unhappy marriage, while voraciously reading Byron and planning her own memoirs. By the time she returned to her parents a year later, she could no longer accept their ambitions for her as either a respectable government worker or upwardly mobile marriage material. Fortunately, they had enough faith in her abilities to send her to Copenhagen to train as a piano teacher.

Her move to the capital city was the catalyst for Michaëlis's creative energies. Her teacher, Victor Bendix—pianist, composer, and conductor—was a powerful and nurturing guide to the world of art and culture. Although he assessed her musical talent as mediocre, he encouraged her to write and convinced her father to let her remain in Copenhagen past the allotted time. In

FOREWORD

1895 Michaëlis met and married the author Sophus
Michaëlis, who also supported her literary ambitions. In
their first years together she published two volumes of
short stories, which were lauded by critics, including the
prominent Georg Brandes, as exhibiting great talent,
though one abused by her choice of sordid subjects. Un-
deterred, Michaëlis expanded her writing to include re-
views, some of which were published under her
husband's name. The joint success of the Michaëlises
brought them into contact with such established writers
as Herman Bang and Bjornson, who became their
friends and mentors.

After the volumes of short stories, Karin
Michaëlis wrote a novel of medieval life, *The Judge*. In
1902, when her third novel, *The Governor*, was published and vilified by the critics, she decided to send
her newly completed work, *The Child*, to Peter Nansen
at Gyldendal's, one of Scandinavia's most distinguished
publishers. Nansen's deeply felt understanding of the
novel sparked a powerfully influential and long-lasting
friendship. In her memoirs Michaëlis attributes her
continuing creative urges to her desire to be with Nansen, if only for consultation. His promotion of *The Child*,
published in the United States as *Andrea*, made it an
international success, leading to translations into six-
teen languages. The novel concerns a young girl who is
dying from the aftereffects of an accident. In a story
that could easily have yielded to conventional senti-
mentality, the protagonist welcomes death as an escape
from the oppression of adult life as reflected in her parents' grim, loveless relationship. It struck such a sympathetic chord that Michaëlis was accused by some

FOREWORD

readers of having stolen the diaries of their dead daughters. Michaëlis's interest in the psychology of young girls and women persisted in such novels as *Lillemor, The Destiny of Ulla Fangel,* and *The Young Mrs. Jonna,* while *The Monk Is Loose upon the Meadows* revealed her satirical bent.

During this period of success Karin and Sophus celebrated their happiness by working and traveling together. Their relationship seems to have been built on a mutual respect for different working styles and the need for individual privacy. Karin Michaëlis recalled that "[e]ach of us even tried to give the other access to the workshop of his mind. But there at the threshold we stopped" (*Little Troll,* 119). Sophus was a successful poet and playwright whose play *A Revolutionary Wedding* was a great success in Europe and in New York. Despite their closeness and compatibility, however, Karin Michaëlis continued to crave the independence of her rebellious girlhood. When she realized that Sophus was infatuated with a beautiful young woman, her independent spirit, combined with her lingering feeling of homeliness, drove her to take a conflicted course of action. She encouraged the affair by going away but used the period of her absence to weigh the possibility of divorce. Although the affair did end, reconciliation was impossible for the obdurate Karin Michaëlis.

The belief in a child's need for independence that had shaped Michaëlis's rebellious spirit forged a lifelong friendship with Eugenia Schwarzwald, founder of a school in Vienna based on antiauthoritarian principles. The school's curriculum emphasized the application of children's individual talents to academic study.

FOREWORD

Michaëlis expressed her admiration for it in her book
The School of Happiness, in which she relates stories about
children along with memories of her own childhood.
The book also formulates her belief in sexual equality.
She argues that, not only should Schwarzwald have
been awarded a prominent place in the cultural affairs of
her country, but women ought to be accepted as scientists, explorers, and captains of industry. However, if a
young woman shows more talent in domestic work than
in any other she should be encouraged to marry and de-
velop "her naturally given femininity."

Michaëlis's decisions did not always prove to
further her own creative and sexual desires. In 1911, on
a sea voyage home from visiting her sisters, Harriet and
Alma, in New York, she indulged her vanity in a passion
that would end in a protractedly unhappy marriage. Always self-deprecating about her physical attractiveness,
she responded powerfully to the ardent pursuit of
Charles Strangeland, an American academic economist,
and married him. Mercurial and possessive, Strangeland
grew jealous of his wife's career while accusing her of
spoiling his. Because he could not find work in Denmark, the home so essential to his wife's creativity and
personal identity, the couple lived apart except for brief
but turbulent reunions. The marriage ended in divorce
after World War I.

It may have been the acute sense of self-sacrifice Michaëlis associated with her second marriage that
she allegorized in a play she wrote in 1914, just as World
War I broke out and Strangeland was demanding that
she abandon her name, now world-famous, and assume
his. *Mother's Eyes* is about a blind Danish woman whose

children emigrate to America. They write of their success and desire to have her visit them, although they know this is impossible because of her blindness. Secretly, she has surgery to restore her sight and sails for New York. Wearing dark glasses on her arrival, she sees her son and daughter standing on the pier in rags. They had deceived her to keep her from worrying. The mother sells her property, gives the proceeds to her children, and dies without telling them the truth about her restored vision.

During World War I, Michaëlis spent considerable time in Vienna, where she explored the possibility of writing a book about wartime conditions. With her friend Eugenia Schwarzwald, she visited refugee camps, where food and fuel were so scarce that hunger and cold was the norm. Michaëlis's politics were driven by a fierce sense of individual responsibility. Recognizing structural and institutional wrongs, she believed in the efficacy of personal intervention. When a German friend defended the absence of Jewish officers in a German officers' club by asserting that it was natural for Jewish officers to leave when no one spoke to them, Michaëlis ended the friendship. When she learned that Gabriele D'Annunzio had refused to relinquish the Italian estate and manuscripts of the German art historian Henry Thode after the war, she prevented D'Annunzio from receiving the Nobel Prize. Never impressed by power and authority, Michaëlis personally challenged the policies of Czech president Tomáš Masaryk concerning the lack of German instruction in the largely German-populated Sudeten schools. After an initial angry outburst, Masaryk later admitted that she was right and changed the official language in each district to that of the majority of its inhabitants.

In the interwar years Michaëlis gave public lectures on such subjects as "Love, Marriage, and Divorce." Using her own experiences and those of her friends as data, she entranced audiences with her ironic sense of the imperatives and infamies of intimate relationships and the laws governing them. She believed that there had to be economic equality in marriage and that this could be established by a common fund out of which joint expenses were paid, with each partner having nothing to say about the other's spending habits. Such a plan, she felt, would foster marital harmony, especially since she believed that economic inequality was a primary cause of marital discord. She devised her plan in response to seeing women degraded by economic dependence and impoverished by miserly divorce settlements. Although she did not campaign for women's rights, Michaëlis felt that women's independence could be fostered early by their parents. Insurance policies purchased at birth would assure women an education that would then provide them with economic self-sufficiency. Then, if their marriages failed, they would not need to ask their ex-husbands for support; if widowed, they would also be protected.

Michaëlis's personal politics proved her morally courageous on countless occasions. Branded by Hitler as "a dangerous woman," she continued to lecture in Nazi-occupied countries, her dais surrounded by gestapo. When Hitler came to power, Michaëlis opened her home at Thurø to those fleeing imprisonment and death. Some she already knew, such as Bertolt Brecht and his wife, Helene Weigel; others were strangers except for their shared political sympathies. Michaëlis reported that many of these refugees had been tortured and then released only as object lessons to other writers. She often heard them screaming in their sleep.

Once it became clear that Denmark was in danger of invasion, Michaëlis left for the United States, where she remained during the war years. Although she enjoyed the vibrant cultural life of New York City and being with her sister Alma and her husband, life became difficult when she found herself cut off from her European publishing income and faced with the short memories of American editors and publishers. Although seven of her books had appeared in the United States, she could not interest publishers in translating and printing her Bibi books, by now classics in Europe. It was only on her return to Denmark that she was able to resume her career.

Still in her prime after the Second World War, Michaëlis was recognized by a younger generation of European writers as a powerful influence. After a meeting with Colette, who was being honored at an Authors' Union banquet in Vienna, she received a basket of flowers from the French writer with a note saying, "If it were not for your books, I could not have written mine" (*Little Troll*, 284). Although Michaëlis attributed this homage to French gallantry, it is clear from the Danish writer's studies of female psychology that she had indeed been a model for the younger writer.

In her last years Michaëlis lived at her home on the island of Thurø, harassed by poverty. Although her books had sold in the millions, she had given away

much of her earnings to others whom she felt were more
needy.

*   *   *

The writings of Karin Michaëlis are varied and
wide-ranging in genre. In addition to her novels for children and adults, she wrote short stories, essays, and re-
views. She produced about seventy titles in book form
alone. Although she did not consider herself a feminist,
she delivered scathing critiques of contemporary atti-
tudes toward women in all of her interviews and magazine articles. Although she agreed with one interviewer,
William Salisbury, that "woman likes to be dominated
by man," she also pointed out that women were relent-
lessly victimized by the "amorous attentions" of em-
ployers, not to mention fathers and brothers (*Twentieth
Century Magazine*, October 1911, 588). In two sequential
articles in *Munsey's Magazine* (April–September 1913),
entitled "Why Are Women Less Truthful Than Men?"
she attributed women's lies both to the complexities of
their nature and to their prescribed societal roles. In
their role as primary care-givers, she felt that women lie
to preserve domestic harmony. Invoking Ibsen's *A Doll's
House*, Michaëlis interpreted Nora's forgery as a selfless
act motivated by her woman's sensitivity to what others
need and feel. Such empathy develops a woman's social
consciousness, "which is independent of laws enacted
to support social order. She is exactly the opposite of
man. She judges from the motive, not from the deed"
(186).

In the second of these articles Michaëlis
ascribed woman's nature to an evolutionary historical

process marked even at the beginning by oppressive inequality. As long as "[t]here was only one opinion, one will—his . . . [w]hat wonder that she shaped her being in accordance with his wishes . . . and without a murmur allowed him to control her whole existence! . . . Her submission and obedience were a cloak beneath which she concealed her own living, suffering ego. And deep within this ego was a world which the husband never entered, aye, whose existence he never even suspected—a world of gardens filled with the fair flowers of dreams and longings . . ." (343).

Here Michaëlis speaks to our contemporary concerns. How do men and women achieve parity in public and private relationships and spaces when we are torn between believing, on the one hand, that men's natures are essentially aggressive and women fundamentally caring or, on the other, that femininity and masculinity are the products of social and cultural pressures? As in our time, when Freud's theories are attracting both intense interest and intense criticism, so in hers Michaëlis followed his exploration of the psychosexual determination of character yet found it necessary to trace women's characters through alternative possibilities.

*   *   *

The literary culture in which Karin Michaëlis lived and worked was, of course, Scandinavian and European. Denmark, in particular, prided itself on sharing Europe's cultural heritage while celebrating a millennium of political and artistic independence. For Danish writers, major European trends such as Romanticism and the Baroque served to enhance the epic and folkloric forms that expressed their cultural history. A new critical perspective on the cultural past and present was initiated by Georg Brandes (1842–1927), a critic and teacher who advocated sociopsychological aproaches to literature in the form of naturalism, thus paving the way for Ibsen's social criticism. In the 1890s, however, protest against Brandes's theories led to a resurgence of lyricism that elevated regionalism over what were considered his cosmopolitan and socialist interests.

Scandinavian women writers of the late nineteenth and early twentieth centuries combined folkloric and symbolic forms with social criticism to focus on the conditions of women's lives. Among these was Amalie Skram (1846–1905), whose 1892 novel *Betrayed* was the first in Norway to deal openly with the destructiveness of a double sexual standard among middle-class men and women. Her taut symbolic structure exposes the acute sexual fears of a seventeen-year-old bride as she wields her destructive defenses against her worldly but increasingly defenseless husband. In Denmark in 1912, Marie Bregendahl (1867–1940) published a novel, *A Night of Death*, that portrayed working-class people authentically and sympathetically.

In many of her novels Karin Michaëlis combines the children's perspective authorized by Hans Christian Andersen with the social criticism advocated by Georg Brandes. By the time she wrote *The Dangerous Age*, such experimentation was becoming widespread throughout Europe in various forms of modernism, and Denmark, closest of the Scandinavian countries to western European culture, had already been affected. Although the most radical experiments in form and syntax are usually recognized as having occurred after the First World War in the writings of Eliot, Joyce, and Rilke, traditional narrative points of view were already being challenged in Gertrude Stein's *Three Lives* (1909). *The Dangerous Age* combines the symbolic and socially critical aspects of Scandinavian traditions and transforms them by introducing a new kind of narrative voice. Dispensing with the "scientific" observations of an omniscient narrator, the novel authenticates subjectivity in the form of a woman's voice that becomes the medium of social critique. Michaëlis had already shown her understanding of the female psyche in *The Child*, but whereas in Denmark the child's perspective was a beloved cultural artifact, that of a middle-aged woman was not even considered worth noting, much less recording.

Most unsettling to contemporary readers of *The Dangerous Age* was its depiction of menopause, a topic completely suppressed even at a time when revelations about human sexuality were becoming standard fare among European modernists, and Scandinavian writers in particular. Although the word *menopause* is never mentioned in the novel, symptoms attributed at the time to the biological bases of middle-aged women's psychological upheavals resonate throughout the narrative. Presented as a spontaneous, unself-conscious experience, Elsie Lindtner's emotional swings produced equally intense and spontaneous defensive reactions in readers. In an otherwise favorable review, May Bateman, writing for *The Fortnightly* (June 7, 1911), noted: "The poignant truth of it makes you want to hide your eyes at times, as you do when a friend is making some piteous confession which you fear she may regret some day, a confession which incidentally lays bare every half-healed wound of your own" (112). Perhaps because there is no narrator to editorialize and provide contexts, judgments, or sympathy, critics took it upon themselves to diagnose Elsie's malaise. George Middleton judged her desire for solitude "hysterical" (179), while the anonymous reviewer for the *New York Times* (Sept. 3, 1911) attributed it to an underlying hope that the young architect who has loved her "will follow her to her lair, haul her forth after the manner of the cave man and carry her away in triumph" (530).

Although the *Athenaeum*'s review (Sept. 30, 1911) warned readers against regarding Elsie as a victim of "neurasthenia and hysteria," it also interpreted her condition as aberrant and perhaps abhorrent to her contemporary society. "A woman who has arrived at that 'dangerous age' when physical beauty comes and goes intermittently, threatening a final departure" suffers from "the common confusion between mental sympathy and sexual feeling." Given the prevailing view that women's middle years represent the onset of an irreversible mental and physical decline, Elsie's sexual yearnings could only be judged as opprobrious. Once her significant life passages were over, the natural stance for the woman of a "certain age" was dignified resignation, not an energetic course of self-discovery that could include a sexual odyssey. Highlighting Elsie's turn away from conventional expectations is the fact of her childlessness. Especially as women of her culture and class were valued most highly as mothers, Elsie's lack of children forced her to focus exclusively on what her life had meant, and what it could come to mean, to herself alone.

Part of what makes *The Dangerous Age* such compelling reading is the unabashed bravura of Elsie's voice. Not only has Michaëlis done away with a traditional narrator who predicts, interprets, and judges her characters, she has undercut the conventional role of the psychologist in this profoundly psychological novel. Elsie is no one's patient but her own; she transforms the private, privileged covenant between psychoanalyst and analysand into a public discourse that links her experiences and fantasies to those of other women. Her narrative thus serves as a woman's self-analysis, acting upon and reacting to, layering and unlayering the social and sexual history of women's lives that so often leads them to a crisis in midlife.

Through Elsie's responses to her own and other women's experiences, Michaëlis offers a revisionary social-psychological model of women's midlife. Rather than identifying their midlife problems as the onset of decline, she presents women's "hysteria" as a symptom of the female character unhinged, in flux, and struggling to reroute the sexual desire that had been deadened by the marriage of convenience. Elsie's decision to leave her "golden cage" validates the imprisonment of every woman in the novel in a system that materializes her as a sexual object. Like those of all the women she knows, Elsie's character is fixed in youth when she realizes that in order to achieve a secure place in society she must wear a "mask" that attracts the highest bidder precisely because he gets what he bargained for—a woman who will become exactly what he wants her to be because she herself has no way of knowing who or what she really is. Of course, at the heart and core of this unknown creature is her sexuality. Repressed in her efforts to have "pretended to be moved by genuine passion," sexuality "bursts free" at the very moment when she is supposed to be free of it—the onset of old age.

The Dangerous Age is a very different novel from Kate Chopin's *The Awakening* (1896), to which it can so easily be compared. Whereas Edna Pontellier discovers her sexuality outside of an empty marriage and suffocating life, the sexuality of all the female characters in *The Dangerous Age* remains a problematic extension of the social processes that have limited them in so many ways. In her representation of these processes Michaëlis suggests that neither the stable order of marriage nor the dangerous adventure of romantic love is a fulfilling pathway for women's sexuality. Chopin condemns these myths by having Edna escape into death. Michaëlis is equally critical, but leaves her novel open to other considerations.

Although all of Elsie Lindtner's women friends suffer through unhappy marriages, it is only at midlife that they discover in themselves a desperate desire that remains unsatisfied—indeed unfocused—despite their involvements in romantic love affairs and even brief encounters. Part of what is so extraordinary about this novel is its suggestion of the existence of other needs for intimacy than those enacted in the plot of any conventional romance. Underlying the distance from her women friends that Elsie establishes through her angry, often patronizing advice is her desire for close, empathetic relations. The "concealed" but "ineradicable hostility"

FOREWORD

that prevails between the sexes in Elsie's world is only
made bearable by women's mutual understanding and
identification. Not that women's relations are harmonious, but as Elsie's conflicted feelings toward her maid,
Jeanne, ultimately reveal, there is the possibility for intimacy here that could produce a sense of a real, un-
masked self that women can value. And yet every
sequence in which Elsie ruminates about women's relations, even her epiphanic scene with Jeanne, ends with
questions. The struggle to deal with these questions
about who and what a woman needs to find herself is
ongoing and, as the novel's open ending suggests, as yet
unresolved, and therefore still compelling to us today.

The conjunction of midlife malaise and thwarted sexuality forecasts two issues that still concern us.
The novel draws constant attention to definitions of and
distinctions between "sex" and "gender" while explor-
ing relationships among women and between men and
women. In lending credence to the biological causes of
menopausal disturbances, Michaëlis would seem to en-
trap women in an inevitable and irreversible decline that
men are able to escape—witness forty-something Richard Lindtner's engagement to a nineteen-year-old debu-
tante. However, the opportunity for Elsie, Lillie, and
Jeanne to test the outer limits of their potential through
other kinds of relationships counterbalances the sense of
biological determinism. Elsie's own combination of resolve and turbulence calls into question any essentialist
arguments that would either hallow women's nurturing
ability or lament their instability.

Still, we must remember that Michaëlis was
writing in the context of a long history of medical atti-

tudes toward women's midlife as well as one in which scientific "discoveries" were having dramatic impact. Persisting into her time were views from the eighteenth century. John Leake, in his 1777 book *Chronic or Slow Diseases Peculiar to Women*, noted such menopausal symptoms as "pain and giddiness of the head, hysteric disorders . . . and a female weakness often very troublesome to others" due to "the many excesses introduced by luxury and the irregularities of the passion." In his introduction comparing *The Dangerous Age* to an 1848 novel about menopause by Octave Feuillet (*La Crise*), Marcel Prévost notes that this subject "is also a dangerous one": "We have made considerable advances since 1848. Even in Denmark physiology now plays a large part in literature" (14). How ironic that the biological view should have been considered an advance when it produced in women an acceptance of the body's decline and therefore an acute fear of aging! Michaëlis corroborates the basis for such fear in her foreword to the 1923 edition of *The Dangerous Age*: "The woman always has a hard time. Her physique brings this about." Once her reproductive years were over, so was a woman's attractiveness. That *The Dangerous Age* continued to be a revelation in the midst of scientific conclusions is attested to by G. Stanley Hall in his 1922 study, *Senescence: The Last Half of Life*, where he applauds Michaëlis's complete emancipation from "a man's point of view . . . in depicting the psychological processes that attend the beginnings of old age in women" (28–29).

    In her memoir, *Little Troll*, Michaëlis recalls how the idea for the novel came from her being haunted by "the strange behavior of several middle-aged women" (139). Their obsessions with cleanliness, sudden miserliness, and extramarital sexual activity produced such outcomes as divorce or incarceration in mental hospitals. Not only were these behaviors unrelated, but the only trait the women shared was age: all were between forty and fifty years old. Although a friend in his seventies tried to dissuade Michaëlis from writing the novel on the ground that no man would be interested in a work "whose main character is an old woman over forty," she was newly inspired by hearing of a woman who had divorced her husband for no other reason than that she "longed for some years of contemplation and meditation" (140–41). Michaëlis's fictional transformation of this rational—indeed sedate—motive contrasts dramatically with the judgment of women's behavior by the medical and legal establishments as hysterical and aberrant. Nevertheless, Michaëlis was accused of being a traitor to her sex. In response, she defended the novel in lectures throughout western Europe. According to her own testimony, she was booed by crowds so angry that she felt in danger. Interestingly, while women were denying that the novel represented anything real about menopause, doctors endorsed it; and as a result of the public debates, punishments for crimes committed during the period Michaëlis had dubbed "the dangerous age" were lightened by some European legislatures.

The Dangerous Age remains gripping because of the way it sustains the tension among competing arguments about "women's natures." Like Elsie's fluctuating moods, the novel defies many conventional dicta. Elsie's diary and letters challenge the reader's reliance on the customary narrative transitions and internal consistencies within characters and in the plot found in other novels of psychological realism. Consistent only with Elsie's experience of herself during this "dangerous" period of her life, the novel also defies neatly compartmentalized diagnoses of women's midlife. Taken together, Elsie's character and her forms of expression invite readers to understand her experience, not as moving progressively or regressively toward resolution of her midlife crisis, but as a continuation of her youth and a "crisis" only in the sense that previously repressed feelings finally explode, demanding recognition.

Works Consulted

Special thanks to Norma Farquhar for her valuable suggestions.

Anderson, Bonnie S., and Judith P. Zinsser. *A History of Their Own: Women in Europe*. Vol. 2. New York: Harper & Row, 1988.

Ardis, Ann. *New Women, New Novels: Feminism and Early Modernism*. New Brunswick, N.J.: Rutgers University Press, 1990.

Clareus, Ingrid, ed. *Scandinavian Women Writers: An Anthology from the 1880s to the 1980s*. Westport, Conn.: Greenwood Press, 1989.

Claudi, Jorgen. *Contemporary Danish Authors*. Copenhagen: Det Danske Selskab, 1952.

Dahlsgard, Inga. *Women in Denmark, Yesterday and Today*. Copenhagen: Det Danske Selskab, 1980.

Fabricius, Susanne. "Preservation of the Childlike in the Writing of Karin Michaelis." Translated by Eric Wagner. In *From Child to Woman* [Fra Barn til Kvinne], edited by Anne-Cathrine Anderson et al. Oslo: Universitets forlaget, 1980.

Farquhar, Norma. Review of "*Bente Rosenbeck, Kvindekon, Den Moderne Kvindeligheds Historie 1880–1980* [The female sex: The history of modern femininity]. *Scandinavian Studies* 62 (Summer 1990): 378–79.

WORKS CONSULTED

Garton, Janet, ed. *Facets of European Modernism*. Norwich: University of East Anglia Press, 1985.

Hall, G. Stanley. *Senescence: The Last Half of Life*. New York: Appleton, 1922.

Matthews, Karen. "Presidential Address," American Psychosomatic Society, Santa Fe, New Mexico, March 1991. Unpublished.

Michaëlis, Karin. *The Dangerous Age: Letters and Fragments from A Woman's Diary*. Introduction by Marcel Prévost. London: John Lane, 1911.

————. *Elsie Lindtner*. Translated by Beatrice Marshall. London: John Lane, 1912.

————, in collaboration with Lenore Sorsby. *Little Troll*. New York: Creative Age Press, 1946.

Mitchell, P. M. *A History of Danish Literature*. Copenhagen: Gyldendal, 1957.

Showalter, Elaine. *A Literature of Their Own: British Women Novelists from Brontë to Lessing*. Princeton, N.J.: Princeton University Press, 1977.

Skram, Amalie. *Betrayed*. Translated by Aileen Hennes. London: Pandora, 1986.

Triden, André. "Karin Michaëlis." *New York Times*, July 16, 1911, 6:9.

The Dangerous Age

M Y DEAR LILLIE,
Obviously it would have been the right thing to give you my news in person—apart from the fact that I should then have enjoyed the amusing spectacle of your horror! But I could not make up my mind to this course.

All the same, upon my word of honour, you, dear innocent soul, are the only person to whom I have made any direct communication on the subject. It is at once your great virtue and defect that you find everything that everybody does quite right and reasonable—you, the wife eternally in love with her husband; eternally watching over your children like a brood-hen.

You are really virtuous, Lillie. But I may add that you have no reason for being anything else. For you, life is like a long and pleasant day spent in a hammock under a shady tree—your husband at the head and your children at the foot of your couch.

You ought to have been a mother stork, dwelling in an old cart-wheel on the roof of some peasant's cottage.

For you, life is fair and sweet, and all humanity angelic. Your relations with the outer world are calm and equable, without temptation to any passions but such as are perfectly legal. At eighty you will still be the virtuous mate of your husband.

Don't you see that I envy you? Not on account of your husband—you may keep him and welcome! Not on account of your lanky maypoles of daughters—for I have not the least wish to be five times running a mother-in-law, a fate which will probably overtake you. No! I envy your superb balance and your imperturbable joy in life.

I am out of sorts to-day. We have dined out twice running, and you know I cannot endure too much light and racket.

We shall meet no more, you and I. How strange it will seem. We had so much in common besides our portly dressmaker and our masseuse with her shiny, greasy hands! Well, anyhow, let us be thankful to the masseuse for our slender hips.

I shall miss you. Wherever you were, the atmosphere was cordial. Even on the summit of the Blocksberg, the chillest, barest spot on earth, you would impart some warmth.

Lillie Rothe, dear cousin, do not have a fit on reading my news: *Richard and I are going to be divorced*.

Or rather, we *are* divorced.

Thanks to the kindly intervention of the Minister of Justice, the affair was managed quickly and without fuss, as you see. After twenty-two years of married life, almost as exemplary as your own, we are going our separate ways.

You are crying, Lillie, because you are such a kind, heaven-sent, tender-hearted creature. But spare your tears. You are really fond of me, and when I tell you that all has happened for the best, you will believe me, and dry your eyes.

There is no special reason for our divorce.

None at least that is palpable, or explicable, to the world. As far as I know, Richard has no entanglements; and I have no lover. Neither have we lost our wits, nor become religious maniacs. There is no shadow of scandal connected with our separation beyond that which must inevitably arise when two middle-aged partners throw down the cards in the middle of the rubber.

It has cost my vanity a fierce struggle. I, who made it such a point of honour to live unassailable and pass as irreproachable. I, who am mortally afraid of the judgment of my fellow creatures—to let loose the gossips' tongues in this way!

I, who have always maintained that the most wretched *ménage* was better than none at all, and that an unmarried or divorced woman had no right to expect more than the semi-existence of a Pariah! I, who thought divorce between any but a very young couple an unpardonable folly! Here am I, breaking a union that has been completely harmonious and happy!

You will begin to realize, dear Lillie, that this is a serious matter.

For a whole year I delayed taking the final step; and if I hesitated so long before realizing my intention, it was partly in order to test my own feelings, and partly for practical reasons; for I *am* practical, and I could not fancy myself leaving my house in the Old Market Place without knowing where I was going to.

My real reason is so simple and clear that few will be content to accept it. But I have no other, so what am I to do?

You know, like the rest of the world, that Richard and I have got on as well as any two people of opposite sex ever can do. There has never been an angry word between us. But one day the impulse—or whatever you like to call it—took possession of me that I must live alone—quite alone and all to myself. Call it an absurd idea, an impossible fancy; call it hysteria—which perhaps it is—I must get right away from everybody and everything.

THE DANGEROUS AGE

It is a blow to Richard, but I hope he will soon get over it. In the long run his factory will make up for my loss.

We concealed the business very nicely. The garden party we gave last week was a kind of "farewell performance." Did you suspect anything at all? We are people of the world and know how to play the game . . . !

If I am leaving to-night, it is not altogether because I want to be "over the hills" before the scandal leaks out, but because I have an indescribable longing for solitude.

Joergen Malthe has planned and built a little villa for me—without having the least idea I was to be the occupant.

The house is on an island, the name of which I will keep to myself for the present. The rooms are fourteen feet high, and the dining-room can hold thirty-six guests. There are only two reception-rooms. But what more could a divorced woman of my age require? The rest of the house—the upper storey—consists of smaller rooms, with bay-windows and balconies. My bedroom, isolated from all the others, has a glass roof, like a studio. Another of my queer notions is to be able to look up from my bed and see the sky above me. I think it is good for the nerves, and mine are in a terrible condition.

So in future, having no dear men, I can flirt with the little stars in God's heaven.

Moreover, my villa is remarkable for its beautiful situation, its fortress-like architecture, and—please make a note of this—its splendid inhospitality. The garden hedge which encloses it is as high as the wall of the women's penitentiary at Christianshafen. The gates are never open, and there is no lodge-keeper. The forest adjoins the garden, and the garden runs down to the water's edge. The original owner of the estate was a crank who lived in a hut, which was so overgrown with moss and creepers that I did not pull it down. Never in my life has anything given me such delight as the anticipation of this hermit-like existence. At the same time, I have engaged a first-rate cook, called Torp, who seems to have the cookery of every country as pat as the Lord's Prayer. I have no intention of living upon bread and water and virtue.

I shall manage without a footman, although I have rather a weakness for menservants. But my income will not permit of such luxuries; or rather I have no idea how far my money will go. I should not care to accept Richard's generous offer to make me a yearly allowance.

I have also engaged a housemaid, whose name is Jeanne. She has the most wonderful amber-coloured eyes, flaming red hair, and long, pointed fingers, so well kept that I cannot help wondering where she got them from. Torp and Jeanne will make the sum-total of my society, so that I shall have every opportunity of living upon my own inner resources.

Dear Lillie, do all you can to put a stop to the worst and most disgusting gossip, now you know the true circumstances of the case. One more thing, in profound confidence, and on the understanding that you will not say a word about it to my husband: Joergen Malthe, dear fellow, formerly honoured me with his youthful affections—as you all knew, to your great amusement. Probably, like a true man, he will be quite frantic when he hears of my strange retirement. Be a little kind and friendly to the poor boy, and make him understand that there is no mystical reason for my departure.

Later on, when I have had time to rest a little, I shall be delighted to hear from you; although I foresee that five-sixths of the letters will be about your children, and the remaining sixth devoted to your husband—whereas I would rather it was all about yourself, and our dear town, with its life and strife. I have not taken the veil; I may still endure to hear echoes of all the town gossip.

If you were here, you would ask what I proposed to do with myself. Well, dear Lillie, I have not left my frocks nor my mirror behind me. Moreover, time has this wonderful property that, unlike the clocks, it goes of itself without having to be wound up. I have the sea, the forest; my piano, and my house. If time really hangs heavy on my hands, there is no reason why I should not darn the linen for Torp!

Should it happen by any chance—which God forbid—that I were struck dead by lightning, or succumbed to a heart attack, would you, acting as my cousin, and closest friend, undertake to put my belongings in order? Not that you would find things in actual disorder; but all the same there would be a kind of semi-order. I do not at all fancy the idea of Richard routing among my papers now that we are no longer a married couple.

With every good wish,

Your cousin,

ELSIE LINDTNER.

MY DEAR, KIND FRIEND, AND FORMER HUSBAND,

Is there not a good deal of style about that form of address? Were you not deeply touched at receiving, in a strange town, flowers sent by a lady? If only the people understood my German and sent them to you in time!

For an instant a beautiful thought flashed through my mind: to welcome you in this way in every town where you have to stay. But since I only know the addresses of one or two florists in the capitals, and I am too lazy to find out the others, I have given up this splendid folly, and simply note it to my account as a "might-have-been."

Shall I be quite frank, Richard? I am rather ashamed when I think of you, and I can honestly say that I never respected you more than to-day. But it could not have been otherwise. I want you to concentrate all your will-power to convince yourself of this. If I had let myself be persuaded to remain with

35

you, after this great need for solitude had laid hold upon me, I should have worried and tormented you every hour of the day.

Dearest and best friend, there is some truth in these words, spoken by I know not whom: "Either a woman is made for marriage, and then it practically does not matter to whom she is married, she will soon understand how to fulfil her destiny; or she is unsuited to matrimony, in which case she commits a crime against her own personality when she binds herself to any man."

Apparently, I was not meant for married life. Otherwise I should have lived happily for ever and a day with you—and you know that was not the case. But you are not to blame. I wish in my heart of hearts that I had something to reproach you with—but I have nothing against you of any sort or kind.

It was a great mistake—a cowardly act—to promise you yesterday that I would return if I regretted my decision. I *know* I shall never regret it. But in making such a promise I am directly hindering you. . . . Forgive me, dear friend . . . but it is not impossible that you may some day meet a woman who could become something to you. Will you let me take back my promise? I shall be grateful to you. Then only can I feel myself really free.

When you return home, stand firm if your friends overwhelm you with questions and sympathy. I should be deeply humiliated if anyone—no matter who—were to pry into the good and bad times we have shared together. Bygones are bygones, and no one can actually realise what takes place between two human beings, even when they have been onlookers.

Think of me when you sit down to dinner. Henceforward eight o'clock will probably be my bedtime. On the other hand I shall rise with the sun, or perhaps earlier. Think of me, but do not write too often. I must first settle down tranquilly to my new life. Later on, I shall enjoy writing you a condensed account of all the follies which can be committed by a woman who suddenly finds herself at a mature age complete mistress of her actions.

Follow my advice, offered for the twentieth time: go on seeing your friends; you cannot

do without them.   Really there is no need for
you to mourn for a year with crape on the
chandeliers and immortelles around my portrait.

You have been a kind, faithful, and deli-
cate-minded friend to me, and I am not so
lacking in delicacy myself that I do not ap-
preciate this in my inmost heart.   But I cannot accept your generous offer to give me
money.   I now tell you this for the first time,
because, had I said so before, you would have
done your best to over-persuade me.   My
small income is, and will be, sufficient for my
needs.

The train leaves in an hour.   Richard, you
have your business and your friends—more
friends than anyone I know.   If you wish me
well, wish that I may never regret the step
I have taken.   I look down at my hands that
you loved—I wish I could stretch them out to
you. . . .

A man must not let himself be crushed.   It
would hurt me to feel that people pitied you.
You are much too good to be pitied.

Certainly it would have been better if, as

you said, one of us had died. But in that case you would have had to take the plunge into eternity, for I am looking forward with joy to life on my island.

For twenty years I have lived under the shadow of your wing in the Old Market Place. May I live another twenty under the great forest trees, wedded to solitude.

How the gossips will gossip! But we two, clever people, will laugh at their gossip.

Forgive me, Richard, to-day and always, the trouble I have brought upon you. I would have stayed with you if I could. Thank you for all. . . .

ELSIE.

That my feeling for you should have died, is quite as incomprehensible to me as to you. No other man has ever claimed a corner of my heart. In a word, having considered the question all round, I am suffering simply from a nervous malady—alas! it is incurable!

My dear Malthe,

We two are friends, are we not, and I think we shall always remain so, even now that fate has severed our ways? If you feel that you have any good reason for being angry with me now, then, indeed, our friendship will be broken; for we shall have no further opportunity of becoming reconciled.

If at this important juncture I not only hid the truth from you, but deliberately misled you, it was not from any lack of confidence in you, or with the wish to be unfriendly. I beg you to believe this. The fact that I cannot even now explain to you my reasons for acting thus makes it all the more difficult to justify my conduct to you. Therefore you must be contented to take my word for it. Joergen Malthe, I would gladly confide in you, but it is impossible. Call it madness, or what you will, but I cannot allow any human being to penetrate my inner life.

THE DANGEROUS AGE

You will not have forgotten that September evening last year, when I spoke to you for the first time about one of my friends who was going to separate from her husband, and who, through my intervention, asked you to draw the plan of a villa in which she might spend the rest of her days in solitude? You entered so completely into this idea of a solitary retreat that your plan was almost perfect. Every time we met last year we talked about the "White Villa," as we called it, and it pleased us to share this little secret together. Nor were you less interested in the interior of the house; in making sketches for the furniture, and arranging the decorations. You took a real delight in this task, although you were annoyed that you had no personal knowledge of your client. You remember that I said to you sometimes in joke: "Plan it as though it were for me"; and I cannot forget what you replied one day: "I hate the idea of a stranger living in the house which I planned with you always in my mind."

Judge for yourself, Malthe, how painful it was to leave you in error. But I could not speak out then, for I had to consider my husband. For this reason I avoided meeting you during the summer; I found it impossible to keep up the deception when we were face to face.

It is I—I myself—who will live in the "White Villa." I shall live there quite alone.

It is useless for me to say, "Do not be angry." You would not be what you are if you were not annoyed about it.

You are young, life lies before you. I am old. In a very few years I shall be so old that you will not be able to realise that there was a time when I was "the one woman in the world" for you. I am not harping on your youth in order to vex you—your youth that you hate for my sake! I know that you are not fickle; but I know, too, that the laws of life and the march of time are alike inexorable.

When I enter the new home you have planned for me, a lonely and divorced woman, I shall think of you every day, and my thoughts will speak more cordial thanks than I can set down coldly in black and white on this paper.

THE DANGEROUS AGE

I do not forbid you to write to me, but, save for a word of farewell, I would prefer your silence. No letters exchanged between us could bring back so much as a reflection of the happy hours we have spent together. Hours in which we talked of everything, and chiefly of nothing at all.

I do not think we were very brilliant when we were together; but we were never bored. If my absence brings you suffering, disappointment, grief—lose yourself in your work, so that in my solitude I may still be proud of you.

You taught me to use my eyes, and there is much, much in the world I should like to see, for, thanks to you, I have learnt how beautiful the world is. But the wisest course for me is to give myself up to my chosen destiny. I shut the door of my "White Villa"—and there my story ends.

Your
ELSIE LINDTNER.

Reading through my letter, it seems to me cold and dry. But it is harder to write such a letter to a dear friend than to a stranger.

LANDED ON MY ISLAND.

CREPT INTO MY LAIR.

THE first day is over. Heaven help me through those to come! Everything here disgusts me, from the smell of the new woodwork and the half-dried wallpapers to the pattering of the rain over my head.

What an idiotic notion of mine to have a glass roof to my bedroom! I feel as though I were living under an umbrella through which the water might come dripping at any moment. During the night this will probably happen. The panes of glass, unless they are very closely joined together, will let the water through, and I shall awake in a pool of water.

Awake, indeed! If only I ever get to sleep! My head aches and burns from sheer fatigue, but I have not even thought of getting into bed yet.

44

For the last year I have had plenty of time to think things over, and now I am at a loss to understand why I have done this. Suppose it is a piece of stupidity—a carefully planned and irrevocable folly? Suppose my irritable nerves have played a trick upon me? Suppose . . . suppose . . .

I feel lonely and without will power. I am frightened. But the step is taken, and I can never turn back. I must never let myself regret it.

This constant rain gives me an icy, damp feeling down my back. It gets on my nerves.

What shall I come to, reduced to the society of two females who have nothing in common with me but our sex? No one to speak to, no one to see. Jeanne is certainly attractive to look at, but I cannot converse with her. As to Torp, she suits her basement as a gnome suits his mountain cave. She looks as though she was made to repopulate a desert unaided. She wears stays that are crooked back and front.

Never in all my life have I felt so disappointed, and compelled to put a good face upon a bad business, as when I splashed through the wet garden and entered the empty house where there was not even a flower to welcome my arrival. The rooms are too large and bare. . . . Why did I not think of that before?

All the same, decorum must be maintained, and my entry was not undignified.

Ah, the rain, the rain! Jeanne and Torp are still cleaning up. They mean to go on half the night, scrubbing and sweeping as though we expected company to-morrow. I start unpacking my trunk, take out a few things and stop—begin again and stop again, horrified at the quantity of clothes I've brought. It would have been more sensible to send them to one of our beloved "charity sales." They are of no use or pleasure now. Black merino and a white woollen shawl— what more do I want here?

God knows how I wish at the present moment I were back in the Old Market Place, even if I only had Richard's society to bore me.

What am I doing here? What do I want

here? To cry, without having to give an account of one's tears to anyone?

Of course, all this is only the result of the rain. I was longing to be here. It was not a mere hysterical whim. No, no. . . .

It was my own wish to bury myself here.

* * *

Yesterday I was all nerves. To-day I feel as fresh and lively as a cricket.

We have been hanging the pictures, and made thirty-six superfluous holes in the new walls. There is no way of concealing them. (I must write to Richard to have my engravings framed.) It would be stretching a point to say we are skilled picture-hangers; we were nearly as awkward as men when they try to hook a woman's dress for her. But the pictures were hung somehow, and look rather nice now they are up.

But why on earth did I give Torp my sketch of "A Villa by the Sea" to hang in her kitchen? Was I afraid to have it near me? Or was it some stupid wish to hurt *his* feelings? *His* only gift. . . . I feel ashamed of myself.

Jeanne has arranged flowers everywhere, and that helps to make the house more home-like.

The place is mine, and I take possession of it. Now the sun is shining. I find pleasure in examining each article of furniture and re-membering the days when we discussed the designs together. I ought not to have let him do all that. It was senseless of me.

* * *

They are much to be envied who can pass away the time in their own society. I am in my element when I can watch other people blowing soap-bubbles; but to blow them my-self. . . .

I am not really clever at creating comfort-able surroundings. Far from it. My white villa always looks uninhabited, in spite of all the flowers with which I allow Jeanne to decorate the rooms. Is it because everything smells so new? Or because there are no old smells? Here there are no whiffs of dust, smoke, or benzine, nor anything which made the Old Market Place the Old Market Place. Everything is so clean here that one hesitates to move a step. The boards are as shiny as though they were polished silver. . . . This very moment Torp appeared in felt shoes and implored me to get her a strip of oilcloth to save her kitchen floor. I feel just the same; I scarcely dare defile this spotless pitchpine.

* * *

What is the use of all these discussions and articles about the equality of the sexes, so long as we women are at times the slaves of an inevitable necessity? I have suffered more than ever the last few days, perhaps because I was so utterly alone. Not a human being to speak to. Yes, I ought to have stayed in bed if only to conceal my ugliness. In town I was wise. But here . . .

* * *

All the same I am proud of my self-control. Many women do not possess as much.

THE DANGEROUS AGE

The moon is in her first quarter; a cold dry wind is blowing up; it makes one cough merely to hear it whistle.

I hate winds of all kinds, and here my enemy seems to have free entry. I ought to have built my house facing south and in some hollow sheltered from the wind. Unfortunately it looks to the north, straight across the open sea.

I have not yet been outside the garden. I have made up my mind to keep to this little spot as long as possible. I shall get accustomed to it. I *must* get accustomed to it.

Dear souls, how they worry me with their letters. Only Malthe keeps silence. Will he deign to answer me?

Jeanne follows me with her eyes as though she wanted to learn some art from me. What art?

Good heavens, what can that girl be doing here?

She does not seem made for the celibate life of a desert island. Yet I cannot set up a footman to keep her company. I will not have men's eyes prying about my house, I have had enough of that.

A manservant—that would mean love affairs, squabbles, and troubles; or marriage, and a change of domestics. No, I have a right to peace, and I will secure it. The worst that could happen to me would be to find myself reduced to playing whist with Jeanne and Torp. Well, why not?

Torp spends all her evenings playing patience on the kitchen window-sill. Perhaps she is telling her fortune and wondering whether some good-looking sailor will be wrecked on the shores of her desert island.

Meanwhile Jeanne goes about in silk stockings. This rather astonishes me. Lillie reproved me for the pernicious custom. Are they a real necessity for Jeanne, or does she know the masculine taste so well?

* * *

From all the birch trees that stand quivering around the house a golden rain is falling. There is not a breath of wind, but the leaves keep dropping, dropping. This morning I stood on the little balcony and looked out over the forest. I do not know why or wherefore, but such a sense of quiet came over me. I seemed to hear the words: "and behold it was very good." Was it the warm russet tint of the trees or the profound perfume of the woods that induced this calm?

All day long I have been thinking of Malthe, and I feel so glad I have acted as I have done. But he might have answered my letter.

Jeanne has discovered the secret of my hair. She asked permission to dress it for me in the evening when my hair is "awake." She is quite an artist in this line, and I let her occupy herself with it as long as she pleased. She pinned it up, then let it down again; coiled it round my forehead like a turban; twisted it into a Grecian knot; parted and smoothed it down on each side of my head like a hood. She played with it and arranged it a dozen different ways like a bouquet of wild flowers.

My hair is still my pride, although it is

losing its gloss and colour. Jeanne said, by way of consolation, that it was like a wood in late autumn. . . .

I should like to know whether this girl sprang from the gutter, or was the child of poor, honest parents. . . .

* * *

"Thousands of women may look at the man they love with their whole soul in their eyes, and the man will remain as unmoved as a stone by the wayside. And then a woman will pass by who has no soul, but whose artificial smile has a mysterious power to spur the best of men to painful desire. . . ."

One day I found these words underlined in a book left open on my table. Who left it there, I cannot say; nor whether it was underlined with the intention of hurting my feelings, or merely by chance.

* * *

I sit here waiting for my mortal enemy. Will he come gliding in imperceptibly or stand suddenly before me? Will he overcome me, or shall I prove the stronger? I am prepared—but is that sufficient?

Torp is really too romantic! To-day it pleased her to decorate the table with virginia creeper. Virginia creeper festooned the hanging lamp; virginia creeper crept over the cloth. Even the joint was decked out with wine-red leaves, until it looked like a ship flying all her flags on the King's birthday. Amid all this pomp and ceremony, I sat all alone, without a human being for whom I might have made myself smart. I, who for the last twenty years, have never even dressed the salad without at least one pair of eyes watching me toss the lettuce as though I was performing some wonderful Indian conjuring trick.

A festal board at which one sits in solitary grandeur is the dreariest thing imaginable.

I rather wish Torp had less "style," as she calls it. Undoubtedly she has lived in large establishments and has picked up some habits and customs from each of them. She is welcome to wait at table in white cotton gloves and to perch a huge silk bow on her hair, which is redolent of the kitchen, but when it comes to trimming her poor work-worn nails to the fashionable pyramidal shape—she really becomes tragic.

She "romanticises" everything. I should not be at all surprised if some day she decked her kitchen range with wreaths of roses and hung up works of art between the stewpans.

I am really glad I did not bring Samuel the footman with me. He could not have waited on me better than Jeanne, and at any rate I am free from his eyes, which, in spite of all their respectful looks, always reminded me of a fly-paper full of dead and dying flies.

Jeanne's look has a something gliding and subtle about it that keeps me company like a witty conversation. It is really on her account that I dress myself well. But I cannot converse with her. I should not like to try, and then to be disillusioned.

Men have often assured me that I was the only woman they could talk with as though I were one of themselves. Personally I never feel at one with menkind. I only understand and admire my own sex.

In reality I think there is more difference between a man and a woman than between an inert stone and a growing plant. I say this . . . I who . . .

* * *

What business is it of mine? We were not really friends. The fact of her having confided in me makes no demands on my feelings. If this thing had happened five years ago, I should have taken it as a rather welcome sensation—nothing more. Or had I read in the paper "On the — inst., of heart disease, or typhoid fever," my peace of mind would not have been disturbed for an hour.

I have purposely refrained from reading the papers lately. Chancing to open one to-day, after a month's complete ignorance of all that had been happening in the world, I saw the following headline: Suicide of a Lady in a Lunatic Asylum.

And now I feel as shaken as though I had

taken part in a crime; as though I had had some share in this woman's death.

I am so far to blame that I abandoned her at a moment when it might still have been possible to save her. . . . But this is a morbid notion! If a person wants "to shuffle off this mortal coil" it is nobody's duty to prevent her.

To me, Agatha Ussing's life or death are secondary matters; it is only the circumstances that trouble me.

Was she mad, or no? Undoubtedly not more insane than the rest of us, but her self-control snapped like a bowstring which is overstrained. She saw—so she said—a grinning death's head behind every smiling face. Merely a bee in her bonnet! But she was foolish enough to talk about it; and when people laughed at her words with a good-natured contempt, her glance became searching and fixed as though she was trying to convince herself. Such an awful look of terror haunted her eyes, that at her gaze a cold shiver, born of one's own fears and forebodings, ran through one.

She compelled us to realise the things we scarcely dare foresee. . . .

I shall never forget a letter in which she wrote these words in a queer, faltering handwriting:

"If men suspected what took place in a woman's inner life after forty, they would avoid us like the plague, or knock us on the head like mad dogs."

Such a philosophy of life ended in the poor woman being shut up in a madhouse. She ought to have kept it to herself instead of posting it up on the walls of her house. It was quite sufficient as a proof of her insanity.

I cannot think what induced me to visit her in the asylum. Not pure pity. I was prompted rather by that kind of painful curiosity which makes a patient ask to see a limb which has just been amputated. I wanted to look with my own eyes into that shadowy future which Agatha had reached before me.

What did I discover? She had never cared for her husband; on the contrary she had betrayed him with an effrontery that would hardly have been tolerated outside the smart world; yet now she suffered the torments of hell from jealousy of her husband. Not of her lovers; their day was over; but of him, because he was the one man she saw. Also because she bore his name and was therefore bound to him.

On every other subject she was perfectly sane. When we were left alone together she said: "The worst of it is that I know my 'madness' will only be temporary. It is a malady incident to my age. One day it will pass away. One day I shall have got through the inevitable phase. But how does that help me now?"

No, it was no more help to her than the dreadful paint with which she plastered her haggard features.

It was not the least use to her. . . .

Her death is the best thing that could have happened, for her own sake and for those belonging to her. But I cannot take my thoughts off the hours which preceded her end; the time that passed between the moment when she decided to commit suicide until she actually carried out her resolve.

* * *

"If men suspected . . ."

It may safely be said that on the whole surface of the globe not one man exists who really knows a woman.

They know us in the same way as the bees know the flowers; by the various perfumes they impart to the honey. No more.

How could it be otherwise? If a woman took infinite pains to reveal herself to a husband or a lover just as she really is, he would think she was suffering from some incurable mental disease.

A few of us indicate our true natures in hysterical outbreaks, fits of bitterness and suspicion; but this involuntary frankness is generally discounted by some subtle deceit.

Do men and women ever tell each other the truth? How often does that happen? More often than not, I think, they deal in half-lies, hiding this, embroidering that, fact.

Between the sexes reigns an ineradicable hostility. It is concealed because life has to be lived, because it is easier and more convenient to keep it in the background; but it is always there, even in those supreme moments when the sexes fulfil their highest destiny.

A woman who knows other women and understands them, could easily prove this in so many words; and every woman who heard her—provided they were alone—would confess she was right. But if a man should join in the conversation, both women would stamp truth underfoot as though it were a venomous reptile.

Men can be sincere both with themselves and others; but women cannot. They are corrupted from birth. Later on, education, intercourse with other women and finally marriage, corrupt them still more.

A woman may love a man more than her own life; may sacrifice her time, her health, her existence to him. But if she is wholly a woman, she cannot give him her confidence.

She cannot, because she dares not.

In the same way a man—for a certain length of time—can love without measure. He can then be unlocked like a cabinet full of secret drawers and pigeonholes, of which we hold the keys. He discloses himself, his present and his past. A woman, even in the closest bonds of love, never reveals more of herself than reason demands.

Her modesty differs entirely from that of a male. She would rather be guilty of incest than reveal to a man the hidden thoughts which sometimes, without the least scruple, she will confide to another woman. Friendship between men is a very different thing. Something honest and frank, from which consequently they withdraw without anger, mutual obligation, or fear. Friendship between women is a kind of masonic oath; the breaking of it a mutual crime. When two women friends quarrel, they generally continue to carry deadly weapons against each other, which they are only restrained from using by mutual fear.

There *are* honest women. At least we believe there are. It is a necessary part of our belief. Who does not think well of mother or sister? But who *believes entirely* in a mother or a sister? Absolutely and unconditionally? Who has never caught mother or sister in a falsehood or a subterfuge? Who has not sometimes seen in the heart of mother or sister, as by a lightning flash, an abyss which the profoundest love cannot bridge over?

Who has ever really understood his mother or sister?

The human being dwells and moves alone. Each woman dwells in her own planet formed of centrifugal fires enveloped in a thin crust of earth. And as each star runs its eternal course through space, isolated amid countless myriads of other stars, so each woman goes her solitary way through life.

It would be better for her if she walked barefoot over red-hot ploughshares, for the pain she would suffer would be slight indeed compared to that which she must feel when, with a smile on her lips, she leaves her own youth behind and enters the regions of despair we call "growing old," and "old age. . . ."

All this philosophizing is the result, no doubt, of having eaten halibut for lunch; it is a solid fish and difficult to digest.

Perhaps, too, having no company but Jeanne and Torp, I am reduced to my own aimless reflections.

Just as clothes exercise no influence on the majority of men, so their emotional life is not much affected by circumstances. With us women it is otherwise. We really *are* different women according to the dresses we wear. We assume a personality in accord with our costume. We laugh, talk and act at the caprice of purely external circumstances.

Take for instance a woman who wants to confide in another. She will do it in quite a different way in broad daylight in a drawing-room than in her little "den" in the gloaming, even if in both cases she happens to be quite alone with her confidante.

If some women are specially honoured as the recipients of many confidences from their own sex, I am convinced they owe it more to physical than moral qualities. As there are some rooms of which the atmosphere is so cosey and inviting that we feel ourselves at home in them without a word of welcome, so we find certain women who seem to be endowed with such receptivity that they invite the confidences of others.

The history of smiles has never yet been written, simply because the few women capable of writing it would not betray their sex. As to men, they are as ignorant on this point as on everything else which concerns women—not excepting love.

I have conversed with many famous women's doctors, and have pretended to admire their knowledge, while inwardly I was much amused at their simplicity. They know how to cut us open and stitch us up again—as children open their dolls to see the sawdust with which they are stuffed and sew them up afterwards with a needle and thread. But they get no further. Yes—a little further perhaps. Possibly in course of time they begin to discover that women are so infinitely their superiors in falsehood that their wisest course is to appear once and for all to believe them then and there. . . .

Women's doctors may be as clever and sly as they please, but they will never learn any of the things that women confide to each other. It is inevitable. Between the sexes lies not only a deep, eternal hostility, but the unfathomable abyss of a complete lack of reciprocal comprehension.

For instance, all the words in a language will never express what a smile will express —and between women a smile is like a masonic sign; we can use them between ourselves without any fear of their being misunderstood by the other sex.

Smiles are a form of speech with which we alone are conversant. Our smiles betray our instincts and our burdens; they reflect our virtues and our inanity.

But the cleverest women hide their real selves behind a factitious smile.

Men do not know how to smile. They look more or less benevolent, more or less pleased, more or less love-smitten; but they are not pliable or subtle enough to smile. A woman who is not sufficiently prudent to mask her features, gives away her soul in a smile. I have known women who revealed their whole natures in this way.

No woman speaks aloud, but most women smile aloud. And the fact that in so doing we unveil all our artifice, all the whirlpool of our inmost being to each other, proves the extraordinary solidarity of our sex.

When did one woman ever betray another?

This loyalty is not rooted in noble sentiment, but proceeds rather from the fear of betraying ourselves by revealing things that are the secret common property of all womanhood.

And yet, if a woman could be found willing to reveal her entire self? . . .

I have often thought of the possibility, and at the present moment I am not sure that she would not do our sex an infinite and eternal wrong.

We are compounded so strangely of good and bad, truth and falsehood, that it requires the most delicate touch to unravel the tangled skein of our natures and find the starting point.

No man is capable of the task.

During recent years it has become the fashion for notorious women to publish their reminiscences in the form of a diary. But has any woman reader discovered in all this literature a single intimate feature, a single frank revelation of all that is kept hidden behind a thousand veils?

If indeed one of these unhappy women ventured to write a plain, unvarnished, but poignant, description of her inner life, where would she find a publisher daring enough to let his name appear on the cover of the book?

I once knew a man who, stirred by a good and noble impulse, and confident of his power, endeavoured to "save" a very young girl whom he had rescued from a house of ill-fame. He took her home and treated her like a sister. He lavished time and confidence upon her. His pride at the transformation which took place in her passed all bounds. The girl was as grateful as a mongrel and as modest as the bride in a romantic novel. He then resolved to make her his wife. But one fine day she vanished, leaving behind her a note containing these words: "Many thanks for your kindness, but you bore me."

During the whole time they had lived together, he had not grasped the faintest notion of the girl's true nature; nor understood that to keep her contented it was not sufficient to treat her kindly, but that she required some equivalent for the odious excitements of the past.

* * *

All feminine confessions—except those between relations which are generally commonplace and uninteresting—assume a kind of beauty in my eyes; a warmth and solemnity that excuses the casting aside of all conventional barriers.

I remember one day—a day of oppressive heat and the heavy perfume of roses—when, with a party of women friends, we began to talk about tears. At first no one ventured to speak quite sincerely; but one thing led to another until we were gradually caught in our own snares, and finally we each gave out something that we had hitherto kept concealed within us, as one locks up a deadly poison.

Not one of us, it appeared, ever cried because of some imperative inward need. Tears are nature's gift to us. It is our own affair whether we squander or economise their use.

Of all our confessions Sophie Harden's was the strangest. To her, tears were a kind of erotic by-play, which added to the enjoyment of conjugal life. Her husband, a good-natured creature, always believed he was to blame, and she never enlightened him on the point.

Most of the others owned that they had recourse to tears to work themselves up when they wanted to make a scene. But Astrid Bagge, a gentle, quiet housewife and mother, declared she kept all her troubles for the evenings when her husband dined at the volunteer's mess, because he hated to see anyone crying. Then she sat alone and in darkness and wept away the accumulated annoyances of the week.

When it came to my turn, I spoke the truth by chance when I said that, however much I wanted to cry, I only permitted myself the luxury about once in two years. I think my complexion is a conclusive proof that my words were sincere.

There are deserts which never know the refreshment of dew or rain. My life has been such a desert.

I, who like to receive confidences, have a morbid fear of giving them. Perhaps it is because I was so much alone, so self-centred, in my childhood.

The more I reflect upon life, the more clearly I see that I have not laid out my talents to the best advantage. I have no sweet memories of infidelity; I have lived irreproachably—and now I am very tired.

I sit here and write for myself alone. I know that no one else will ever read my words; and yet I am not quite sincere, even with myself.

Life has passed me by; my hands are empty; now it is too late.

Once happiness knocked at my door, and I, poor fool, did not rise to welcome it.

I envy every country wench or servant girl who goes off with a lover. But I sit here waiting for old age.

Astrid Bagge. . . . As I write her name, I feel as though she were standing weeping behind my back; I feel her tears dropping on my neck. I cannot weep—but how I long for tears!

* * *

Autumn! Torp has made a huge fire of logs in the open grate. The burning wood gives out an intoxicating perfume and fills the house with cosey warmth. For want of something better to do I am looking after the fire myself. I carefully strip the bark from each log before throwing it on the flames. The smell of burning birch-bark goes to my head like strong wine. Dreams come and go.

Joergen Malthe, what a mere boy you are!

* * *

The garden looks like a neglected churchyard, forgotten of the living. The virginia creeper falls in blood-red streamers from the verandah. The snails drag themselves along in the rain; their slow movements remind me of women *enceinte*. The hedge is covered with spiders' webs, and the wet clay sticks to one's shoes as one walks on the paths.

Yet there are people who think autumn a beautiful time of year!

* * *

My will is paralysed from self-disgust. I find myself involuntarily listening and watching for the postman, who brings nothing for me. There are moments when my fingers seem to be feeling the smoothness of the cream-laid "At Home" cards which used to be showered upon us, especially at this season. Towards evening I grow restless. Formerly my day was a *crescendo* of activity until the social hours were reached. Now the hours fall one by one in ashes before my eyes.

I am myself, yet not myself. There are moments when I envy every living creature that has the right to pair—either from hate or from habit. I am alone and shut out. What consolation is it to be able to say: "It was my own choice!"

* * *

A letter from Malthe.

No, I will not open it. I do not wish to know what he writes. . . . It is a long letter.

* * *

My nerves are quiet. But I often lie awake, and my sleep is broken. The stars are shining over my head, and I never before experienced such a sense of repose and calm. Is this the effect of the stars, or the letter?

I am forty-two! It cannot be helped. I cannot buy back a single day of my life. Forty-two! But during the night the thought does not trouble me. The stars above reckon by ages, not by years, and sometimes I smile to think that as soon as Richard returns home, the rooms in our house in the Old Market will be lit up, and the usual set will assemble there without me.

The one thing I should like to know is whether Malthe is still in Denmark.

I would like to know where my thoughts should seek him—at home or abroad.

I played with him treacherously when I called him "the youth," and treated him as a mere boy. If we compare our ages it is true enough, but not if we compare feelings.

Can there be anything meaner than for a woman to make fun of what is really sacred to her? My feelings for Malthe were and still are sacred. I myself have befouled them with my mockery.

But when I am lying in my bed beneath the vast canopy of the sky, all my sins seem forgiven me. Fate alone—Fate who bears all things on his shoulders—is to blame, and I wish nothing undone.

The letter will never be read. Never voluntarily by me.

*   *
*

I do not know the day of the week. That is one step nearer the goal for which I long. May it come to pass that the weeks and months shall glide imperceptibly over me, so that I shall only recognise the seasons by the changing tints of the forest and the alternations of heat and cold.

Alas, those days are still a long way off!

I have just been having a conflict with myself, and I find that all the time I have been living here as though I were spending a summer holiday in Tyrol. I have been simply deceiving myself and playing with the hidden thought that I could begin my life over again.

I have shivered with terror at this self-deception. The last few nights I have hardly slept at all. A traveller must feel the same who sails across the sea ignorant of the country to which he journeys. Vaguely he pictures it as resembling his native land, and lands to find himself in a wilderness which he must plant and cultivate until it blossoms with his new desires and dreams. By the time he has turned the desert into a home, his day is over. . . .

* * *

If I could but make up my mind to burn that letter! I weigh it, first in my right hand, then in my left. Sometimes its weight makes me happy; sometimes it fills me with foreboding. Do the words weigh so heavy, or only the paper?

Last night I held it close to the candle.

But when the flame touched my letter, I drew it quickly away.—It is all I have left to me now. . . .

* * *

Richard writes to me that Malthe has been commissioned to build a great hospital. Most of our great architects competed for the work. He goes on to ask whether I am not proud of "my young friend."

My young friend! . . .

* * *

Jeanne spoke to me about herself to-day. I think she was quite bewildered by the extraordinary fall of leaves which has almost blinded us the last three days. She was doing my hair, and tracing a line straight across my forehead, she remarked:

"Here should be a ribbon with red jewels."

I told her that I had once had the same idea, but I had given it up out of consideration for my fellow creatures.

"But there are none here," she exclaimed.

I replied laughing:

"Then it is not worth while decking myself out!"

Jeanne took out the pins and let my hair down.

"If I were rich," she said, "I would dress for myself alone. Men neither notice nor understand anything about it."

We went on talking like two equals, and a few minutes later, remembering what I had observed, I gave her some silk stockings. Instead of thanking me, she remarked so suddenly that she took my breath away:

"Once I sold myself for a pair of green silk stockings."

I could not help asking the question:

"Did you regret your bargain?"

She looked me straight in the face:

"I don't know. I only thought about my stockings."

Naturally such conversations are rather risky; I shall avoid them in future. But the riddle is more puzzling than ever. What brought Jeanne to share my solitude on this island?

Now we have a man about the place. Torp got him. He digs in the garden and chops wood. But the odour impregnates Torp and even reaches me.

He makes eyes at Jeanne, who looks at me and smiles. Torp makes a fuss of him, and every night I smell his pipe in the basement.

* * *

I have shut myself upstairs and played patience. The questions I put to the cards come from that casket of memories the seven keys of which I believed I had long since thrown into the sea. A wretched form of amusement! But the piano makes me feel sad, and there is nothing else to do.

Malthe's letter is still intact. I wander around it like a mouse round a trap of which it suspects the danger. My heart meanwhile yearns to know what words he uses.

He and I belong to each other for the rest of our lives. We owe that to my wisdom. If he never sees me, he will never be able to forget me.

* * *

How could I suppose it for a single moment! There is no possibility of remaining alone with oneself! No degree of seclusion, nor even life in a cell, would suffice. Strong as is the call of freedom, the power of memory is stronger; so that no one can ever choose his society at will. Once we have lived with our kind, and become filled with the knowledge of them, we are never free again.

A sound, a scent—and behold a person, a scene, or a destiny, rises up before us. Very often the phantoms that come thronging around me are those of people whose existence is quite indifferent to me. But they appear all the same—importunate, overbearing, inevitable.

We may close our doors to visitors in the flesh; but we are forced to welcome these phantoms of the memory; to notice them and converse with them without reserve.

People become like books to me. I read them through, turn the pages lightly, annotate them, learn them by heart. Sometimes I am at fault; I see them in a new light. Things that were not clear to me become plain; what was apparently incomprehensible becomes as straightforward as a commercial ledger.

It might be a fascinating occupation if I could control the entire collection of these memories; but I am the slave of those that come unbidden. In the town it was just the reverse; one impression effaced another. I did not realise that thought might become a burden.

* * *

The time draws on. The last few days my nerves have made me feverish and restless; to-day for no special reason I opened and read all my letters, except his. It was like reading old newspapers; yet my heart beat faster with each one I opened.

Life there in the city runs its course, only it has nothing more to do with me, and before long I shall have dropped out of memory like one long dead. All these hidden fears, all this solicitude, these good wishes, preachings and forebodings—there is not a single genuine feeling among the whole of them!

Margethe Ernst is the only one of my old

friends who is sincere and does not let herself be carried away by false sentiment. She writes cynically, brutally even: "An injection of morphia would have had just the same effect on you; but everyone to his own taste."

As to Lillie, with her simple, gushing nature, she tries to write lightly and cheerfully, but one divines her tears between the lines. She wishes me every happiness, and assures me she will take Malthe under her motherly wing.

"He is quiet and taciturn, but fortunately much engrossed with his plans for the new hospital which will keep him in Denmark for some years to come."

His work absorbs him; he is young enough to forget.

As to the long accounts of deaths, accidents and scandals, a year or two ago they might have stirred me in much the same way as the sight of a fire or a play. Now it amuses me quite as much to watch the smoke from my chimney, as it ascends and seems to get caught in the tops of the trees.

Richard is still travelling with his grief, and entertains me scrupulously with accounts of all the sights he sees and of his lonely sleepless nights. Are they always as lonely as he makes out?

As in the past, he bores me with his interminable descriptions and his whole middle-class outlook. Yet for many years he dominated my senses, which gives him a certain hold over me still. I cannot make up my mind to take the brutal step which would free me once and for all from him. I must let him go on believing that our life together was happy.

Why did I read all these letters? What did I expect to find? A certain vague hope stirred within me that if I opened them I should discover something unexpected.

The one remaining letter—shall I ever find courage to open it? I *will* not know what he has written. He does not write well I know. He is not a good talker; his writing would probably be worse. And yet, I look upon that sealed letter as a treasure.

Merely touching it, I feel as though I was in the same room with him.

* * *

Lillie's letter has really done me good; her regal serenity makes itself apparent beneath all she undertakes. It is wonderful that she does not preach at me like the others. "You must know what is right for yourself better than anybody else," she says. These words, coming from her, have brought me unspeakable strength and comfort, even though I feel that she can have no idea of what is actually taking place within me.

Life for Lillie can be summed up in the words, "the serene passage of the days." Happy Lillie. She glides into old age just as she glided into marriage, smiling, tranquil, and contented. Nobody, nothing, can disturb her quietude.

It is so when both body and soul find their repose and happiness in the same identical surroundings.

* * *

Jeanne, with some embarrassment, asked permission to use the bathroom. I gave her leave. It is quite possible that living in the basement is not to her taste. To put a bathroom down there would take nearly a fortnight, and during that time I shall be deprived of my own, for I cannot share my bathroom or my bedroom with anyone, least of all a woman. . . .

I shall never forget the one visit I paid to the Russian baths and the sight of Hilda Bang. Clothed, she presents rather a fine appearance, with a good figure; but seen amid the warm steam, in nature's garb, she seemed horrible.

I would rather walk through an avenue of naked men than appear before another woman without clothes. This feeling does not spring from modesty—what is it?

* * *

How quiet it is here! Only on Wednesdays and Saturdays the steamer for England goes by. I know its coming by the sound of the screw, but I take care never to see it pass.

What if I were seized with an impulse to embark on her. . . .

If one fine morning when Jeanne brought the tea she found the bird flown?

The time is gone by. Life is over.

I am getting used to sitting here and stitching at my seam. My work does not amount to much, but the mechanical movement brings a kind of restfulness.

I find I am getting rather capricious. Between meals I ring two or three times a day for tea—like a convalescent trying a fattening cure. Jeanne attends to my hair with indefatigable care. Without her, should I ever trouble to do it at all?

What can any human being want more than this peace and silence?

* * *

If I could only lose this sense of being empty-handed, all would be well. Yesterday I went down to the seashore and gathered little pebbles. I carried them away and amused myself by taking them up in handfuls. During the night I felt impelled to get up and fetch them, and this morning I awoke with a round stone in each hand.

Hysteria takes strange forms. But who knows what is the real ground of hysteria? I used to think it was the special malady of the unmated woman; but, in later years, I have known many who had had a full share of the passional life, legitimate and otherwise, and yet still suffered from hysteria.

* * *

I begin to realise the fascination of the cloister; the calm, uniform, benumbing existence. But my comparison does not apply. The nun renounces all will and responsibility, while I cannot give up one or the other.

I have reached this point, however: only that which is bounded by my garden hedge seems to me really worthy of consideration. The house in the Old Market Place may be burnt down for all I care. Richard may marry again. Malthe may. . . .

Yes, I think I could receive the news in silence like the monk to whom the prior announces, "One of the brethren is dead, pray

87

for his soul." No one present knows, nor will ever know, whether his own brother or father has passed away.

What hopeless cowardice prevents my opening his letter!

EVENING.

SOMEBODY should found a vast and cheerful sisterhood for women between forty and fifty; a kind of refuge for the victims of the years of transition. For during that time women would be happier in voluntary exile, or at any rate entirely separated from the other sex.

Since all are suffering from the same trouble, they might help each other to make life, not only endurable, but harmonious. We are all more or less mad then, although we struggle to make others think us sane.

I say "we," though I am not of their number—in age, perhaps, but not in temperament. Nevertheless I hear the stealthy footsteps of the approaching years. By good fortune, or calculation, I have preserved my youthful appearance, but it has cost me dear to economise my emotions.

Old age, in truth, is only a goal to be foreseen. A mountain to be climbed; a peak from which to see life from every side—provided we have not been blinded by snowfalls on the way. I do not fear old age; only the hard ascent to it has terrors for me. The day, the hour, when we realise that something has gone from our lives; when the cry of our heart provokes laughter in others!

To all of us women comes a time in life when we believe we can conquer or deceive time. But soon we learn how unequal is the struggle. We all come to it in the end.

Then we grow anxious. Anxious at the coming of day; still more anxious at the coming of night. We deck ourselves out at night as though in this way we could put our anxiety to flight.

We are careful about our food and our rest; we watch that our smiles leave no wrinkles. . . . . Yet never a word of our secret terror do we whisper aloud. We keep silence or we lie. Sometimes from pride, sometimes from shame.

Hitherto nobody has ever proclaimed this great truth: that as they grow older—when the summer comes and the days lengthen—

women become more and more women. Their feminality goes on ripening into the depths of winter.

Yet the world compels them to steer a false course. Their youth only counts so long as their complexions remain clear and their figures slim. Otherwise they are exposed to cruel mockery. A woman who tries late in life to make good her claim to existence, is regarded with contempt. For her there is neither shelter nor sympathy.

It sometimes happens that a winter gale strips all the leaves from a tree in a single night. When does a woman grow old in body and soul in one swift and merciful moment? From our birth we are accursed.

I blame no one for my failure in life. It was in my own hands. If I could live it through again from the start, it is more than probable I should waste the years for a second time.

CHRISTMAS EVE.

A T this hour there will be festivities in the Old Market Place. Richard's last letter touched me profoundly; something within me went out toward his honest nature. . . .

What is the use of all these falsehoods? I long for an embrace. Is that shocking? We women are so wrapped in deceit that we feel ashamed of confessing such things. Yet it is true, I miss Richard. Not the husband or companion, but the lover.

What use in trying to soothe my senses by walking for hours through the silent woods.

Lillie, in the innocence of her heart, sent me a tiny Christmas tree, decorated by herself and her lanky daughters. Sweets and little presents are suspended from the branches. She treats me like a child, or a sick person.

Well, let it be so! Lillie must never have the vexation of learning that I detested her girls simply because they represented the youthful generation which sooner or later must supplant me.

I have made good use of my eyes, and I know what I have seen: the same enmity exists between two generations as between the sexes.

While the young folk in their arrogant cruelty laugh at us who are growing old, we, in our turn, amuse ourselves by making fun of them. If women could buy back their lost youth by the blood of those nearest and dearest to them, what crimes the world would witness!

How I used to hate Richard when I saw him so completely at his ease among young people, and able to take them so seriously.

* * *

Christmas Eve! In honour of Jeanne, I put on one of my very best frocks—Paquin. Moreover, I have decorated myself with rings and chains as though I were a silly Christmas Tree myself.

Jeanne has enjoyed herself to-day. She and Torp rose before it was light to deck the rooms with pine branches. Over the verandah waves the Swedish flag, which Torp generally suspends above her bed, in remembrance of Heaven knows who. I gave myself the pleasure of surprising Jeanne, by bestowing upon her my green *crêpe de Chine*. In future grey and black will be my only wear.

After the obligatory goose, and the inevitable Christmas dishes, I spent the evening reading the letters with which "my friends" honour me punctiliously.

Without seeing the handwriting, or the signature, I could name from the contents alone the writer of each one of them. They all write about the honours which have befallen Joergen Malthe: a hospital here; a palace of archives there. What does it matter to me? I would far rather they wrote: "To-day a motor-car ran over Joergen Malthe and killed him on the spot."

I have arrived at that stage.

But to-night I will not think about him; I would rather try to write to Magna Wellmann. I may be of some use to her. In any case I will tell her things that it will do her good to hear. She is one of those who take life hard.

DEAR MAGNA WELLMANN,
It is with great difficulty that I venture to give you advice at this moment. Besides, we are so completely opposed in habit, thought, and temperament. We have really nothing in common but our unfortunate middle age and our sex; therefore, how can it help you to know what I should do if I were in your place?

May I speak quite frankly without any fear of hurting your feelings? In that case I will try to advise you; but I can only do so by making your present situation quite clear to you. Only when you have faced matters can you hope to decide upon some course of action which you will not afterwards regret. Your letter is the queerest mixture of self-deception and a desire to be quite frank. You try to throw dust in my eyes, while at the same time you are betraying all that you are most anxious to conceal. Judging from your letter, the maternal feeling is deeply ingrained in your nature. You are prepared to fight for your children and sacrifice yourself for them if necessary. You would put yourself aside in order to secure for them a healthy and comfortable existence.

The real truth is that your conscience is pricking you with a remorse that has been instigated by others. Maternal sentiment is not your strong point; far from it. In your husband's lifetime you did not try to make two and two amount to five; and you often showed very plainly that your children were rather an encumbrance than otherwise. When at last your affection for them grew, it was not because they were your own flesh and blood, but because you were thrown into daily contact with these little creatures whom you had to care for.

Now you have lost your head because the outlook is rather bad. Your family, or rather your late husband's people, have attempted to coerce you in a way that I consider entirely unjustifiable. And you have allowed yourself to be bullied, and therefore, all unconsciously, have given them some hold over your life and actions.

THE DANGEROUS AGE

You must not forget that your husband's family, without being asked, have been allowing you a yearly income which permitted you to live in the same style as before Professor Wellmann's death. They placed no restrictions upon you, and made no conditions. Now, the family—annoyed by what reaches their ears—want to insist that you should conform to their wishes; otherwise they will withdraw the money, or take from you the custody of the children. This is a very arbitrary proceeding.

Reflect well what they are asking of you before you let yourself be bound hand and foot.

Are you really capable, Magna, of being an absolutely irreproachable widow?

Perhaps there ought to be a law by which penniless widows with children to bring up should be incarcerated in some kind of nunnery, or burnt alive at the obsequies of their husbands. But failing such a law, I do not think a grown-up woman is obliged to promise that she will henceforth take a vow of chastity. One must not give a promise only to break it, and, my dear Magna, I do not think you are the woman to keep a vow of that kind.

For this reason you ought never to have made yourself dependent upon strangers by accepting their money for the education of your children. At the same time I quite see how hard it would be to find yourself empty-handed with a pack of children all in need of something. If you had not courage to try to live on the small pension allowed by the State, you would have done better to find some means of earning a livelihood with the help of your own people.

You never thought of this; while I was too much taken up with my own affairs just then to have any superfluous energy for other people's welfare or misfortune.

But now we come to the heart of the question. For some years past you have confided in me—more fully than I really cared about. While your husband was alive I often found it rather painful to be always looking at him through the keyhole, so to speak. But this confidence justifies me in speaking quite frankly.

My dear Magna, listen to me. A woman of your temperament ought never to bind herself by marriage to any man, and is certainly not fit to have children. You were intended —do not take the words as an insult—to lead the life of a *fille de joie*. The term sounds ugly—but I know no other that is equally applicable. Your vehement temperament, your insatiable desire for new excitements—in a word, your whole nature tends that way. You cannot deny that your marriage was a grave mistake.

There was just the chance—a remote one —that you might have met the kind of husband to suit you : an eminently masculine type, the kind who would have kept the whip-hand over you, and regarded a wife as half-mistress, half-slave. Even then I think your conjugal happiness would have ceased the first day he lost the attraction of novelty.

Professor Wellmann, your quiet, correct husband, was as great a torment to you as you

were to him. Without intending it, you made
his life a misery. The dreadful scenes which
were brought about by your violent and sen-
sual temperament so changed his disposition
that he became brutal; while to you they became a kind of second nature, a necessity, like
food or sleep.

Magna, you will think me brutal, too, because I now tell you in black and white what
formerly I lacked the courage to say. Believe
me, it was often on the tip of my tongue to
exclaim: "Better have a lover than torment
this poor man whose temperament is so different to your own."

I will not say you did not care for your
husband. You learnt to see his good qualities; but there was no true union between you.
You hated his work. Not like a woman who
is jealous of the time spent away from her;
but because you believed such arduous brain
work made him less ardent as a lover. Although you did not really care for him, you
would have sacrificed all his fame and reputation for an hour of unreasoning passion.

At his death you lost the breadwinner and

the position you had gained in the world as the wife of a celebrity. Your grief was sincere; you felt your loneliness and loss. Then for the first time you clung to your children, and erroneously believed you were moved by maternal feeling. You honestly intended henceforward to live for them alone.

All went well for three months, and then the struggle began. Do you know, Magna, I admired the way you fought. You would not give way an inch. You wore the deepest weeds. Sheltered behind your crape, you surrounded yourself by your children, and fought for your life.

This inward conflict added to your attractions. It gave you an air of nobility you had hitherto lacked.

Then the world began to whisper evil about you while you were still quite irreproachable.

No, after all there *was* something to reproach you with, although it was not known to outsiders. While you were fighting your instincts and trying to live as a spotless widow, your character was undergoing a change: against your will, but not unconsciously, you were become a perfect fury. In this way your children acquired that timidity which they have never quite outgrown. Strangers began to notice this after a while, and to criticise your behaviour.

Time went on. You wrote that you were obliged to do a "cure" in a nursing home for nervous complaints. When I heard this, I could not repress a smile, in spite of your misfortunes. Nerve specialists may be very clever, but can they be expected, even at the highest fees, to replace defunct husbands. You were kept in bed and dosed with bromides and sulphonal. After a few weeks you were pronounced quite well, and left the home a little stouter and rather languid after keeping your bed so long.

When you got home you turned the house upside-down in a frantic fit of "cleaning." You walked for miles; you took to cooking; and at night, having wearied your body out with incessant work, you tried to lull your brain by reading novels.

What was the use of it all? The day you confessed to me that you had walked about the streets all night lest you should kill yourself and your children, I realised that your powers of resistance were at an end. A week later you had embarked upon your first *liaison*. A month later the whole town was aware of it.

That was about a year after the Professor's death. Six or seven years have passed since then, and you have gone on from adventure to adventure, all characterised by the same lamentable lack of discretion. The reason for this lies in your own tendency to self-deception. You want to make yourself and others believe that you are always looking for ideal love and constant ties. In reality your motives are quite different. You hug the traditional conviction that it would be disgraceful to own that your pretended love is only an affair of the senses. And yet, if you had not been so anxious to dupe yourself and others, you might have gone through life frankly and freely.

The night is far advanced, moreover it is Christmas Eve.

I will not accuse you without producing

proofs.   Enclosed you will find a whole series
of letters, dated irregularly, for you only used
to write to me when I was away from home
in the summer.   In these letters, which I have
carefully collected, and for which I have no
ground for reproaching you, you will see
yourself reflected as in a row of mirrors.   Do
not be ashamed; your self-deception is not
your fault; society is to blame.   I am not
sending the letters back to discourage or hurt
you; only that you may see how, with each
adventure, you have started with the same
sentimental illusions and ended with the same
pitiable disenchantment.

A penniless widow turned forty—we are
about the same age—with five children has
not much prospect of marrying again, however attractive she may be.   I have told you
so repeatedly; but your feminine vanity re-
fuses to believe it.   In each fresh adventure
you have seen a possible marriage—not
because you feel specially drawn towards
matrimony, but because you are unwill-
ing to leave the course free to younger
women.

You have shown yourself in public with your admirers.

Neglecting the most ordinary precautions, you have allowed them to come to your house; in a word, you have unblushingly advertised connections which ought to have been concealed.

And the men you selected?

I do not wish to criticise your choice; but I quite understand why your friends objected and were ashamed on your account.

At first people made the best of the situation, tacitly hoping that the affairs might lead to marriage and that your monetary cares would thus find a satisfactory solution. But after so many useless attempts this benevolent attitude was abandoned, and scandal grew.

Meanwhile you, Magna, blind to all opinion, continued to follow the same round: flirtation, sentiment, intimacy, adoration, submission, jealousy, suspicion, suffering, hatred, and contempt.

The more inferior the man of your choice, the more determined you were to invest him with extraordinary qualities. But as soon as the next one appeared on the scene, you began to judge his predecessor at his true value.

If all this had resulted in your getting the wherewithal to bring up your children in comfort, I should say straight out: "My dear Magna, pay no attention to what other people say, go your own road."

But, unfortunately, it is just the reverse; your children suffer. They are growing up. Wanda and Ingrid are almost young women. In a year or two they will be at a marriageable age. How much longer do you suppose you can keep them in ignorance? Perhaps they know things already. I have somtimes surprised a look in Wanda's eyes which suggested that she saw more than was desirable.

In my opinion it is better for children not to find out these things until they are quite old enough to understand them completely. But the evil is done, and cannot be undone. And yet, Magna, the peace of mind of these innocent victims is entirely in your hands. You can secure it without making the sacrifice that your husband's family demands of you.

You have no right to let your children grow up in this unwholesome atmosphere; and the atmosphere with which their dear mother surrounds them cannot be described as healthy.

If your character was as strong as your temperament, you would not hesitate to take all the consequences on your own shoulders. But it is not so. You would shrink from the hard work involved in emigrating and making yourself a new home abroad; at the same time you would be lowered in your own eyes if you gave your children into the care of others.

Then, since for the next few years you will never resign yourself to single life, and are not likely to find a husband, you must so arrange your love affairs that they escape the attention of the world. Why should you mix them up with your home life and your children? What you need are prudence and calculation; but you have neither.

You will never fix your life on a firm basis until you have relegated men to the true place they occupy in your existence. If you could only make yourself see clearly the fallacy of thinking that every man you meet is going to love you for eternity. A woman like yourself can attract lovers by the dozen; but yours is not the temperament to inspire a serious relationship which might become a lasting friendship. If you constantly see yourself left in the lurch and abandoned by your admirers before you have tired of them yourself, it is because you always delude yourself on this point.

I know another woman situated very much as you are. She too has a large family, and a weakness for the opposite sex. Everybody knows that she has her passing love affairs, but no one quarrels with her on that score.

She is really entitled to some respect, for she lives in her own house the life of an irreproachable matron. She shows the tenderest regard for the needs of her children, and never a man crosses her threshold but the doctor.

You see, dear Magna, that I have devoted half my Christmas night to you, which I certainly should not have done if I did not feel a special sympathy for you. If I wind up my letter with a proposal that may wound your feelings at first sight, you must try to understand that it is kindly meant.

Living here alone, a few months' experience has shown me that my income exceeds my requirements, and I can offer to supply you with a sum which you can pay me back in a year or two, without interest. This would enable you to learn some kind of business which would secure you a living and free you from family interference. Consider it well.

I live so entirely to myself on this island that I have plenty of time to ponder over my own lot and that of other people. Write to me when you feel the wish or need to do so. I will reply to the best of my ability. If I am very taciturn about my own affairs, it springs from an idiosyncrasy that I cannot overcome. To make sure of my meaning I have read my letter through once more, and find that it does not express all I wanted to say. Never mind, it is true in the main. Only try to understand that I do not wish to sit in judgment upon you, only to throw some light on the situation. With all kind thoughts.

Yours,

ELSIE LINDTNER.

* * *

It snows, and snows without ceasing. The trees are already wrapped in snow, like precious objects packed in wadding. The paths will soon be heaped up to their level. The snowflakes are as large as daisies. When I go out they flutter round me like a swarm of butterflies. Those that fall into the water disappear like shooting stars, leaving no trace behind.

The glass roof of my bedroom is as heavy as a coffin-lid. I sleep with my window open, and when there comes a blast of wind my eyes are filled with snow. This morning, when I woke, my pillow-case was as wet as though I had been crying all night.

Torp already sees us in imagination snowed up and receiving our food supplies down the chimney. She is preparing for the occasion. Her hair smells as though she had been singe-

ing chickens, and she has illuminated the basement with small lamps and red shades edged
with pearl fringes.

Jeanne is equally enchanted. When she
goes outside without a hat her hair looks like
a burning torch against the snow. She does
not speak, but hums to herself, and walks more
lightly and softly than ever, as though she
feared to waken some sleeper.

. . . I remember how Malthe and I were
once talking about Greece, and he gave me an
account of a snowstorm in Delphi. I cannot
recall a word of his description; I was not
listening, but just thinking how the snow
would melt when it fell upon his head.

He has fulfilled my request not to write. I
have not had a line since his only letter came.
And yet . . .

*   *   *

I have burnt his letter.

I have burnt his letter. A few ashes are all
that remain to me.

It hurts me to look at the ashes. I cannot
make up my mind to throw them away.

I have got rid of the ashes. It was harder than I thought. Even now I am restless.

* * *

I am glad the letter is destroyed. Now I am free at last. My temptations were very natural.

The last few days I have spent in bed. Jeanne is an excellent nurse. She makes as much fuss of me as though I were really ill, and I enjoy it.

* * *

The Nirvana of age is now beginning. In the morning, when Jeanne brushes my hair, I feel a kind of soothing titillation which lasts all day. I do not trouble about dressing; I wear no jewellery and never look in the glass.

Very often I feel as though my thoughts had come to a standstill, like a watch one has forgotten to wind up. But this blank refreshes me.

Weeks have gone by since I wrote in my

diary. Several times I have tried to do so;
but when I have the book in front of me, I
find I have nothing to set down.

In the twilight I sit by the fire like an old
child and talk to myself. Then Torp comes
to me for the orders which she ends by giving
herself, and I let her talk to me about her own
affairs. The other day I got her on the subject of spooks. She is full of ghost stories,
and relates them with such conviction that her
teeth chatter with terror. Happy Torp, to
possess such imagination!

Some days I hardly budge from one position, and can with difficulty force myself to
leave my table; at other times I feel the need
of incessant movement. The forest is very
quiet, scarcely a soul walks there. If I do
chance to meet anyone, we glare at each other
like two wild beasts, uncertain whether to attack or to flee from each other.

The forest belongs to me. . . .

The piano is closed. I never use it now.
The sound of the wind in the trees is music
enough for me. I rise from my bed and

listen until I am half frozen. I, who was never stirred or pleased by the playing of virtuosi!

I have no more desires. Past and future both repose beneath a shroud of soft, mild fog. I am content to live like this. But the least event indoors wakes me from my lethargy. Yesterday Torp sent for the sweep. Catching sight of him in my room, I could not repress a scream. I could not think for the moment what the man could be doing here.

Another time a stray cat took refuge under my table. I was not aware of it, but no sooner had I sat down than I felt surcharged with electricity. I rang for Jeanne, and when she came into the room the creature darted from its hiding-place, and I was panic-stricken.

Jeanne carried it away, but for a long time afterwards I shivered at the sight of her.

Whence comes this horror of cats? Many people make pets of them. Personally I should prefer the company of a boa-constrictor.

* * *

THE DANGEROUS AGE

A man whose vanity I had wounded once took it upon himself to tell me some plain truths. He did me this honour because I had not sufficiently appreciated his attentions.

He assured me that I was neither clever nor gifted, but that I was merely skilful at not letting myself be caught out, and had a certain quickness of repartee. He was quite right.

What time and energy I have spent in trying to keep up this reputation of being a clever woman, when I was really not born one!

My vanity demanded that I should not be run after for my appearance only; so I surrounded myself with clever men and let them call me intellectual. It was Hans Andersen's old tale of "The King's New Clothes" over again.

We spoke of political economy, of statesmanship, of art and literature, finance and religion. I knew nothing about all these things, but, thanks to an animated air of attention, I steered safely between the rocks and won a reputation for cleverness.

* * *

THE DANGEROUS AGE

In English novels, with their insipid sweetness that always reminds me of the smell of frost-bitten potatoes, the heroine sometimes permits herself the luxury of being blind, lame, or disfigured by smallpox. The hero adores her just the same. How false to life! My existence would have been very different if ten years ago I had lost my long eyelashes, if my fingers had become deformed, or my nose shown signs of redness. . . .

A red nose! It is the worst catastrophe that can befall a beautiful woman. I always suspected this was the reason why Adelaide Svanstroem took poison. Poor woman, unluckily she did not take a big enough dose!

* * *

JANUARY.

MY senses are reawakening. Light and sound now bring me entirely new impressions; what I see, I now also feel, with nerves of which hitherto I did not suspect the existence. When evening draws on I stare into the twilight until everything seems to shimmer before my eyes, and I dream like a child. . . .

Yesterday, before going to bed, I went on my balcony, as I usually do, to take a last glance at the sea. But it was the starry sky that fixed my attention. It seemed to reveal and offer itself to me. I felt I had never really seen it before, although I sleep with it over my head!

Each star was to me like a dewdrop created to slake my thirst. I drank in the sky like a plant that is almost dead for want of moisture. And while I drank it in, I was conscious of a sensation hitherto unknown to me. For the first time in my life I was aware of the existence of my soul. I threw back my head to gaze and gaze. Night enfolded me in all its splendour, and I wept.

What matter that I am growing old? What matter that I have missed the best in life? Every night I can look towards the stars and be filled with their chill, eternal peace.

I, who never could read a poem without secretly mocking the writer, who never believed in the poets' ecstasies over Nature, now I perceive that Nature is the one divinity worthy to be worshipped.

* * *

I miss Margarethe Ernst; especially her amusing ways. How she glided about among people, always ready to dart out her sharp tongue, always prepared to sting. And yet she is not really unkind, in spite of her little cunning smile. But her every movement makes a singular impression which is calculated.

We amused each other. We spoke so candidly about other people, and lied so gracefully to each other about ourselves. Moreover, I think she is loyal in her friendship, and of all my letters hers are the best written.

I should have liked to have drawn her out, but she was the one person who knew how to hold her own. I always felt she wore a suit of chain armour under her close-fitting dresses which was proof against the assaults of her most impassioned adorers.

She is one of those women who, without appearing to do so, manages to efface all her tracks as she goes. I have watched her change her tactics two or three times in the course of an evening, according to the people with whom she was talking. She glided up to them, breathed their atmosphere for an instant, and then established contact with them.

She is calculating, but not entirely for her own ends; she is like a born mathematician who thoroughly enjoys working out the most difficult problems.

I should like to have her here for a week.

She, too, dreads the transition years. She tries in vain to cheat old age. Lately she adopted a "court mourning" style of dress,

and wore little, neat, respect-impelling man-
tillas round her thin, Spanish-looking face.
One of these days, when she is close upon fifty,
we shall see her return to all the colours of
the rainbow and to ostrich plumes. She lives
in hopes of a new springtide in life. Shall
I invite her here?

She would come, of course, by the first train,
scenting the air with wide nostrils, like a stag,
and an array of trunks behind her!

No! To ask her would be a lamentable
confession of failure.

* * *

The last few days I have arrived at a
condition of mind which occasions great self-
admiration. I am now sure that, even if the
difference in our ages did not exist, I could
never marry Malthe.

I could do foolish, even mean things for
the sake of the one man I have loved with all
my heart. I could humble myself to be his
mistress; I could die with him. But set up a
home with Joergen Malthe—never!

The terrible part of home life is that every

piece of furniture in the house forms a link in the chain which binds two married people long after love has died out—if, indeed, it ever existed between them. Two human beings—who differ as much as two human beings always must do—are compelled to adopt the same tastes, the same outlook. The home is built upon this incessant conflict. The struggle often goes on in silence, but it is not the less bitter, even when concealed.

How often Richard and I gave way to each other with a consideration masking an annoyance that rankled more than a violent quarrel would have done. . . . What a profound contempt I felt for his tastes; and, without saying it in words, how he disapproved of mine!

No! His home was not mine, although we lived in it like an ideal couple, at one on all points. My person for his money—that was the bargain, crudely but truthfully expressed.

* * *

Just as one arranges the scenery for a *tableau vivant,* I prepared my "living grave" in this house, which Malthe built in ignorance of its future occupant. And here I have learnt that joy of possession which hitherto I have only known in respect of my jewellery.

This house is really my home. My first and only home. Everything here is dear to me, because it *is* my own.

I love the very earthworms because they do good to my garden. The birds in the trees round about the house are my property. I almost wish I could enclose the sky and clouds within a wall and make them mine.

In Richard's house in the Old Market I never felt at home. Yet when I left it I felt as though all my nerves were being torn from my body.

Joergen Malthe is the man I love; but apart from that he is a stranger to me. We do not think or feel alike. He has his world and I have mine. I should only be like a vampire to him. His work would be hateful to me before a month was past. All women in love are like Magna Wellmann. I shudder when I think of the big ugly room where he lives and works; the bare deal table, the dusty books, the trunk covered with a travelling rug, the dirty curtains and unpolished floor.

Who knows? Perhaps the sense of discomfort and poverty which came over me the day I visited his rooms was the chief reason why I never ventured to take the final step. He paced the carpetless floor and held forth interminably upon Brunelleschi's cupola. He sketched its form in the air with his hands, and all the time I was feeling in imagination their touch upon my head. Every word he spoke betrayed his passion, and yet he went on discussing this wretched dome—about which I cared as little as for the inkstains on his table.

I expressed my surprise that he could put up with such a room.

"But I get the sunshine," he said, blushing.

I am quite sure that he often stands at his window and builds the most superb palaces from the red-gold of the sunset sky, and marble bridges from the purple clouds at evening.

Big child that you are, how I love you!

But I will never, never start a home with you!

Well, surely one gardener can hardly suffice to poison the air of the place. If he is a nuisance I shall send him packing.

The man comes from a big estate. If he is content to cultivate my cabbage patch, it must be because, besides being very ugly, he has some undiscovered faults. But I really cannot undertake to make minute inquiries into the psychical qualities of Mr. Under-gardener Jensen.

His photograph was sent by a registry office, among many others. We examined them, Jeanne, Torp, and myself, with as deep an interest as though they had been fashion plates from Paris. To my silent amusement, I watched Torp unconsciously sniffing at each photograph as though she thought smells could be photographed, too.

Prudence prompted me to select this man; he is too ugly to disturb our peace of mind. On the other hand, as I had the wisdom not to pull down the hut in which the former proprietor lived, the two rooms there will have to do for Mr. Jensen, so that we can keep him at a little distance.

THE DANGEROUS AGE

Torp asked if he was to take meals in the kitchen.

Certainly! I have no intention of having him for my opposite neighbour at table. But, on the whole, he had better have his meals in his hut, then we shall not be always smelling him.

* * *

Perhaps we are really descended from dogs, for the sense of smell can so powerfully influence our senses.

I would undertake in pitch darkness to recognise every man I know by the help of my nose alone; that is, if I passed near enough to him to sniff his atmosphere. I am almost ashamed to confess that men are the same to me as flowers; I judge them by their smell. I remember once a young English waiter in a restaurant who stirred all my sensibilities each time he passed the back of my chair. Luckily Richard was there! For the same reason I could not endure Herr von Brincken to come near me—and equally for the same reason Richard had power over my senses.

Every time I bite the stalk of a pansy I recall the neighbourhood of the young Englishman.

Men ought never to use perfumes. The Creator has provided them. But with women it is different. . . .

* * *

To-day is my birthday. No one here knows it. Besides, what woman would enjoy celebrating her forty-third birthday? Only Lillie Rothe, I am sure! . . .

One day I was talking to a specialist about the thousands of women who are saved by medical science to linger on and lead a wretched semi-existence. These women who suffer for years physically and are oppressed by a melancholy for which there seems to be no special cause. At last they consult a doctor; enter a nursing home and undergo some severe operation. Then they resume life as though nothing had happened. Their surroundings are unchanged; they have to fulfil all the duties of everyday life—even the conjugal life is taken up once more. And these poor creatures, who are often ignorant of the nature of their illness, are plunged into despair because life seems to have lost its joy and interest.

I ventured to observe to the doctor with whom I was conversing that it would be better for them if they died under the anæsthetic. The surgeon reproved me, and inquired whether I was one of those people who thought that all born cripples ought to be put out of their misery at once.

I did not quite see the connection of ideas; but I suppressed my desire to close his argument by telling him of an example which is branded upon my memory.

Poor Mathilde Bremer! I remember her so well before and after the operation. She was not afraid to die, because she knew her husband was devoted to her. But she kept saying to the surgeon:

"You must either cure me or kill me. For my own sake and for his, I will not go on living this half-invalidish life."

She was pronounced "cured." Two years later she left her husband, very much against his will, but feeling she was doing the best for both of them.

She once said to me: "There is no torture to equal that which a woman suffers when she loves her husband and is loved by him; a woman for whom her husband is all in all, who longs to keep his devotion, but knows she must fail, because physically she is no longer herself."

The life Mathilde Bremer is now leading —that of a solitary woman divorced from her husband—is certainly not enviable. Yet she admits that she feels far better than she used to do.

* * *

Any one might suppose I was on the way to become a rampant champion of the Woman's Cause. May I be provided with some other occupation! I have quite enough to do to manage my own affairs.

Heaven be eternally praised that I have no children, and have been spared all the ailments which can be "cured" by women's specialists!

* * *

THE DANGEROUS AGE

Ye powers! How interminable a day can be! Surely every day contains forty-eight hours!

I can actually watch the seconds oozing away, drop by drop. . . . Or rather, they fall slowly on my head, like dust upon a polished table. My hair is getting steadily greyer.

It is not surprising, because I neglect it.

But what is the use of keeping it artificially brown with lotions and pomades? Let it go grey!

Torp has observed that I take far more pleasure in good cooking than I did at first.

My dresses are getting too tight. I miss my masseuse.

* * *

To-day I inspected my linen cupboard with all the care of the lady superior of an aristocratic convent. I delighted in the spectacle of the snowy-white piles, and counted it all. I am careful with my money, and yet I like to have great supplies in the house. The more bottles, cases, and bags I see in the larder, the better pleased

I am. In that respect Torp and I are agreed. If we were cut off from the outer world by flood, or an earthquake, we could hold out for a considerable time.

* * *

If I had more sensibility, and a little imagination—even as much as Torp, who makes verses with the help of her hymn-book—I think I should turn my attention to literature. Women like to wade in their memories as one wades through dry leaves in autumn. I believe I should be very clever in opening a series of whited sepulchres, and, without betraying any personalities, I should collect my exhumed mummies under the general title of, "Woman at the Dangerous Age." But besides imagination, I lack the necessary perseverance to occupy myself for long together with other people's affairs.

* * *

We most of us sail under a false flag; but it is necessary. If we were intended to be as transparent as glass, why were we born with our thoughts concealed?

If we ventured to show ourselves as we really are, we should be either hermits, each dwelling on his own mountain-top, or criminals down in the valleys.

* * *

Torp has gone to evening service. Angelic creature! She has taken a lantern with her, therefore we shall probably not see her again before midnight. In consequence of her religious enthusiasm, we dined at breakfast-time. Yes, Torp knows how to grease the wheels of her existence!

Naturally she is about as likely to attend church as I am. Her vespers will be read by one of the sailors whose ship has been laid up near here for the winter. Peace be with her —but I am dreadfully bored.

I have a bitter feeling as though Jeanne and I were doing penance, each in a dark corner of our respective quarters. The Sundays of my childhood were not worse than this.

In the distance a cracked, tinkling bell

"tolls the knell of parting day." Jeanne and I are depressed by it. I have taken up a dozen different occupations and dropped them all.

If it were only summer! I am oppressed as though I were sitting in a close bower of jasmine; but we are in mid-winter, and I have not used a drop of scent for months.

But, after all, Sundays were no better in the Old Market Place. There I had Richard from morning till night. To be bored alone is bad; to be bored in the society of one other person is much worse. And to think that Richard never even noticed it! His incessant talk reminded me of a mill-wheel, and I felt as though all the flour was blowing into my eyes.

* * *

I will take a brisk constitutional.

* * *

What is the matter with me? I am so nervous that I can scarcely hold my pen. I have never seen a fog come on so suddenly; I thought I should never find my way back to the house. It is so thick I can hardly see the nearest trees. It has got into the room, and seems to be hanging from the ceiling. I am damp through and through.

The fire has gone out, and I am freezing. It is my own fault; I ought to have rung for Jeanne, or put on some logs myself, but I could not summon up resolution even for that.

What has become of Torp, that she is staying out half the day? How will she ever find her way home? With twenty lanterns it would be impossible to see ten yards ahead of one. My lamp burns as though water was mixed with the oil.

Overhead I hear Jeanne pacing up and down. I hear her, although she walks so lightly. She too is restless and upset. We have a kind of influence on each other, I have noticed it before.

If only she would come down of her own accord. At least there would be two of us.

I feel the same cold shivers down my back that I remember feeling long ago, when my nurse induced me to go into a churchyard. I thought I saw all the dead coming out of their graves. That was a foggy evening, too. How strange it is that such far-off things return so clearly to the mind.

The trees are quite motionless, as though they were listening for something. What do they hear? There is not a soul here—only Jeanne and myself.

Another time I shall forbid Torp to make these excursions. If she must go to church, she shall go in the morning.

It is very uncanny living here all alone in the forest, without a watch-dog, or a man near at hand. One is at the mercy of any passer-by.

For instance, the other day, some tipsy sailors came and tried the handle of the front-door. . . . But then, I was not in the least frightened; I even inspired Torp with courage.

I have a feeling that Jeanne is sitting up-stairs in mortal terror. I sit here with my pen in my hand like a weapon of defence. If I could only make up my mind to ring. . . .

There, it is done! My hand is trembling like an aspen leaf, but I must not let her see that I am frightened. I must behave as though nothing had happened.

Poor girl! She rushed into the room without knocking, pale as a corpse, her eyes starting from her head. She clung to me like a child that has just awakened from a bad dream.

What is the matter with us? We are both terrified. The fog seems to have affected our wits.

I have lit every lamp and candle, and they flicker fitfully, like Jeanne's eyes.

The fog is getting more and more dense. Jeanne is sitting on the sofa, her hand pressed to her heart, and I seem to hear it beating, even from here.

I feel as though some one were dying near me—here in the room.

Joergen, is it you? Answer me, is it you?

Ah! I must have gone mad. . . . I am not superstitious, only depressed.

All the doors are locked and the shutters barred. There is not a sound. I cannot hear anything moving outside.

It is just this dead silence that frightens us. . . . Yes, that is what it is. . . .

* * *

Now Jeanne is asleep. I can hardly see her through the fog.

She sits there like a shadow, an apparition, and the fog floats over her red hair like smoke over a fire.

I know nothing whatever about her. She is as reserved about her own concerns as I am about mine. Yet I feel as though during this hour of intense fear and agitation I had seen into the depths of her soul. I understand her, because we are both women. She suffers from the eternal unrest of the blood.

She has had a shock to her inmost feelings. At some time or other she has been so deeply wounded that she cannot live again in peace.

She and I have so much in common that we might be blood-relations. But we ought not to live under the same roof as mistress and servant.

* * *

Gradually the fog is dispersing, and the lights burn brighter. I seem to follow Jeanne's dreams as they pass beneath her brow. Her mouth has fallen a little open, as if she were dead. Every moment she starts up; but when she sees me she smiles and drops off again. Good heavens, how utterly exhausted she seems after these hours of fear!

But somebody *is* there! Yes . . . outside . . . there between the trees. . . . I see somebody coming. . . .

It is only Torp, with her lantern, and the dressmaker from the neighbouring village. The moment she opened the basement door and I heard her voice I felt quite myself again.

* * *

We have eaten ravenously, like wolves. For the first time Jeanne sat at table with me and shared my meal. For the first and prob-

ably for the last time. Torp opened her eyes
very wide, but she was careful to make no observations.

My fit of madness to-night has taught me
that the sooner I have a man of some kind to
protect the house the better.

* * *

Jeanne has confided in me. She was too
upset to sleep, and came knocking at my bedroom door, asking if she might come in. I
gave her permission, although I was already
in bed. She sat at the foot of my bed and told
me her story. It is so remarkable that I must
set in down on paper.

Now I understand her nice hands and all
her ways. I understand, too, how it came
about that I found her one day turning over
the pages of a volume by Anatole France, as
though she could read French.

Her parents had been married twelve years
when she was born. When she was thirteen
they celebrated their silver wedding. Until
that moment in her life she had grown up in
the belief that they were a perfectly united

couple. The father was a chemist in a small town, and they lived comfortably. The silver wedding festivities took place in their own house. At dinner the girl drank some wine and felt it had gone to her head. She left the table, saying to her mother, "I am going to lie down in my room for a little while." But on the way she turned so giddy that she went by mistake into a spare room that was occupied by a cavalry officer, a cousin of her mother's. Too tired to go a step farther, she fell asleep on a sofa in the darkened room. A little later she woke, and heard the sounds of music and dancing downstairs, but felt no inclination to join in the gaiety. Presently she dropped off again, and when she roused for the second time she was aware of whispers near her couch. In the first moment of awakening she felt ashamed of being caught there by some of the guests. She held her breath and lay very still. Then she recognized her mother's voice. After a few minutes she grasped the truth. . . . Her mother, whom she worshipped, and this officer, whom she admired in a childish way!

They lit the candles.　She forced herself to lie motionless, and feigned to be fast asleep. She heard her mother's exclamation of horror: "Jeanne!"　And the captain's words:

"Thank goodness she is sleeping like a log!"

Her mother rearranged her disordered hair, and they left the room.

After a few minutes she returned with a lamp, calling out:

"Jeanne, where are you, child?　We have been searching all over the house!"

Her pretended astonishment when she discovered the girl made the whole scene more painful to Jeanne.　But gathering up her self-control as best she could, she succeeded in replying:

"I am so tired: let me have my sleep out."

Her mother bent over her and kissed her several times. The child felt as though she would die while submitting to these caresses.

This one hour, with its cruel enlightenment, sufficed to destroy Jeanne's joy in life for ever. At the same time it filled her mind with impure thoughts that haunted her night and day.

She matured precociously in the atmosphere of her own despair.

There was no one in whom she could confide; alone she bore the weight of a double secret, either of which was enough to crush her youth.

She could not bear to look her mother in the face. With her father, too, she felt ill at ease, as though she had in some way wronged him. Everything was soiled for her. She had but one desire; to get away from home.

About two years later her mother was seized with fatal illness. Jeanne could not bring herself to show her any tenderness. The piteous glance of the dying woman followed all her comings and goings, but she pretended not to see it. Once, when her father was out of the room, her mother called Jeanne to the bedside:

"You know?" she asked.

Jeanne only nodded her head in reply.

"Child, I am dying, forgive me."

But Jeanne moved away from the bed without answering the appeal.

No sooner had the doctor pronounced life

to be extinct than she felt a strange anxiety. In her great desire to atone in some way for her past harshness, the girl resolved that, no matter what befell her, she would do her best to hide the truth from her father.

That night she entered the room where the dead woman lay, and ransacked every box and drawer until she found the letters she was seeking. They were at the bottom of her mother's jewel-case. Quickly she took possession of them; but just as she was replacing the case in its accustomed place, her father came in, having heard her moving about. She could offer no explanation of her presence, and had to listen in silence to his bitter accusation: "Are you so crazy about trinkets that you cannot wait until your poor mother is laid in her grave?"

In the course of that year one of the chemist's apprentices seduced her. But she laughed in his face when he spoke of marriage. Later on she ran away with a commercial traveller, and neither threats nor persuasion would induce her to return home.

After this, more than once she sought in some

fleeting connection a happiness which never came to her. The only pleasure she got out of her adventures was the power of dressing well. When at last she saw that she was not made for this disorderly life, she obtained a situation in a German family travelling to the south of Europe.

There she remained until homesickness drove her back to Denmark. Her complete lack of ambition accounts for her being contented in this modest situation.

She never made any inquiries about her father, and only knows that he left his money to other people, which does not distress her in the least. Her sole reason for going on living is that she shrinks from seeking death voluntarily.

I wonder if there exists a man who could save her? A man who could make her forget the bitterness of the past? She assures me I am the only human being who has ever attracted her. If I were a man she would be devoted to me and sacrifice everything for my sake..

It is a strange case. But I am very sorry

for the girl. I have never come across such a peculiar mixture of coldness and ardour.

When she had finished her story she went away very quietly. And I am convinced that to-morrow things will go on just as before. Neither of us will make any further allusion to the fog, nor to all that followed it.

SPRING.

I AM driven mad by all this singing and playing! One would think the steamboats were driven by the force of song, and that atrocious orchestras were a new kind of motive power. From morning till night there is no cessation from patriotic choruses and folk-songs.

Sometimes The Sound looks like a huge drying-ground in which all these red and white sails are spread out to air.

How I wish these pleasure-boats were birds! I would buy a gun and practise shooting, in the hopes of killing a few. But this is the close season. . . . The principal thoroughfares of a large town could hardly be more bustling than the sea just now—the sea that in winter was as silent and deserted as a graveyard.

People begin to trespass in my forest and to prowl round my garden. I see their inquisitive faces at my gates. I think I must buy a dog to frighten them away. But then I should have to put up with his howling after some dear and distant female friend.

* * *

How that gardener enrages me! His eyes literally twinkle with sneaky thoughts. I would give anything to get rid of him.

But he moves so well! Never in my life have I seen a man with such a walk, and he knows it, and knows too that I cannot help looking at him when he passes by.

Torp is bewitched. She prepares the most succulent viands in his honour. Her French cookery book is daily in requisition, and, judging from the savoury smells which mount from the basement, he likes his food well seasoned.

Fortunately he is nothing to Jeanne, although she does notice the way he walks from his hips, and his fine carriage.

Midday is the pleasantest hour now. Then the sea is quiet and free from trippers. Even the birds cease to sing, and the gardener takes his sleep. Jeanne sits on the verandah, as I

have given her permission to do, with some
little piece of sewing. She is making artificial roses with narrow pink ribbon; a de-
lightful kind of work.

* * *

D<small>EAR</small> P<small>ROFESSOR</small> R<small>OTHE</small>,

Your letter was such a shock to me that I could not answer it immediately, as I should have wished to do. For that reason I sent you the brief telegram in reply, the words of which, I am sorry to say, I must now repeat: "I know nothing about the matter." Lillie has never spoken a word to me, or made the least allusion in my presence, which could cause me to suspect such a thing. I think I can truly say that I never heard her pronounce the name of Director Schlegel.

My first idea was that my cousin had gone out of her mind, and I was astonished that you —being a medical man—should not have come to the same conclusion. But on mature consideration (I have thought of nothing but Lillie for the last two days) I have changed my opinion. I think I am beginning to understand what has happened, but I beg you to remember that I alone am responsible for

what I am going to say. I am only dealing
with suppositions, nothing more.

Lillie has not broken her marriage vows.
Any suspicion of betrayal is impossible, having regard to her upright and loyal nature.
If to you, and to everybody else, she appeared
to be perfectly happy in her married life, it
was because she really was so. I implore you
to believe this.

Lillie, who never told even a conventional
falsehood, who watched over her children
like an old-fashioned mother, careful of what
they read and what plays they saw, how could
she have carried on, unknown to you and to
them, an intrigue with another man? Impossible, impossible, dear Professor! I do not
say that your ears played you false as to the
words she spoke, but you must have put a
wrong interpretation upon them.

Not once, but thousands of times, Lillie has
spoken to me about you. She loved and
honoured you. You were her ideal as man,
husband, and father. She was proud of you.
Having no personal vanity or ambition, like

so many good women, her pride and hopes were all centred in you.

She used literally to become eloquent on the subject of your operations; and I need hardly remind you how carefully she followed your work. She studied Latin in order to understand your scientific books, while, in spite of her natural repulsion from the sight of such things, she attended your anatomy classes and demonstrations.

When Lillie said, "I love Schlegel, and have loved him for years," her words did not mean "And all that time my love for you was extinct."

No, Lillie cared for Schlegel and for you too. The whole question is so simple, and at the same time so complicated.

Probably you are saying to yourself: "A woman must love one man or the other." With some show of reason, you will argue: "In leaving my house, at any rate, she proved at the moment that Schlegel alone claimed her affection."

Nevertheless I maintain that you are wrong.

Lillie showed every sign of a sane, well-balanced nature. Well, her famous equability and calm deceived us all. Behind this serene exterior was concealed the most feminine of all feminine qualities—a fanciful, visionary imagination.

Do you or I know anything about her first girlish dreams? Have you—in spite of your happy life together—ever really understood her innermost soul? Forgive my doubts, but I do not think you have. When a man possesses a woman as completely as you possessed Lillie, he thinks himself quite safe. You never knew a moment's doubt, or supposed it possible that, having you, she could wish for anything else. You believed that you fulfilled all her requirements.

How do you know that for years past Lillie has not felt some longings and deficiencies in her inner life of which she was barely conscious, or which she did not understand?

You are not only a clever and capable man; you are kind, and an entertaining companion; in short, you have many good qualities which Lillie exalted to the skies. But your nature is not very poetical. You are, in fact, rather prosaic, and only believe what you see. Your judgments and views are not hasty, but just and decisive.

Now contrast all this with Lillie's immense indulgence. Whence did she derive this if not from a sympathetic understanding of things which we do not possess? You remember how we used to laugh when she defended some criminal who was quite beyond defence and apology! Something intense and far-seeking came into her expression on those occasions, and her heart prompted some line of argument which reason could not support.

She stood all alone in her sympathy, facing us, cold and sceptical people.

But how she must have suffered!

Then recollect the pleasure it gave her to discuss religious and philosophical questions. She was not "religious" in the common acceptation of the word. But she liked to get to the bottom of things, and to use her imagination. We others were indifferent, or frankly bored, by such matters.

And Lillie, who was so gentle and lacking in self-assertion, gave way to us.

Recall, too, her passion for flowers. She felt a physical pang to see cut flowers with their stalks out of water. Once I saw her buy up the whole stock-in-trade of a flower-girl, because the poor things wanted water. Neither you nor your children have any love of flowers. You, as a doctor, are inclined to think it unhealthy to have plants in your rooms; consequently there were none, and Lillie never grumbled about it.

Lillie did not care for modern music. César Franck bored her, and Wagner gave her a headache. Her favourite instrument was an old harpsichord, on which she played Mozart, while her daughters thundered out Liszt and Rubinstein upon a concert grand, and you, dear Professor, when in a good humour, strode about the house whistling horribly out of tune.

Finally, Lillie liked quiet, musical speech, and she was surrounded by people who talked at the top of their voices.

"Absurd trifles," I can hear you saying. Perhaps. But they explain the fact that although she was happy in a way, she still had many aspirations which were not only unsatis-fied, but which, without meaning it unkindly, you daily managed to crush.

Lillie never blamed others. When she found that you did not understand the things she cared for, she immediately tried to think she was in the wrong, and her well-balanced nature helped her to conquer her own predi-lections.

She was happy because she willed to be happy. Once and for all she had made up her mind that she was the luckiest woman in existence; happy in every respect; and she was deeply grateful to you.

But in the depths of her heart—so deeply buried that perhaps it never rose to the sur-face even in the form of a dream—lay that secret something which led to the present mis-fortune.

I know nothing of her relations with Schlegel, but I think I may venture to say that they were chiefly limited to intercourse of the soul; and for that reason they were so fatal.

Have you ever observed the sound of

Schlegel's voice? He spoke slowly and so softly; I can quite believe it attracted your wife in the beginning; and that afterwards, gradually, and almost imperceptibly, she gravitated towards him. He possessed so many qualities that she admired and missed.

The man is now at death's door, and can never explain to us what passed between them—even admitting that there was anything blameworthy. As far as I know, Schlegel was quite infatuated with a totally different woman. Had he really been in love with Lillie, would he have been contented with a few words and an occasional pressure of her hand? Therefore, since it is out of the question that your wife can have been unfaithful to you, I am inclined to think that Schlegel knew nothing of her feelings for him.

You will reply that in that case it must all be gross exaggeration on Lillie's part. But you, being a man, cannot understand how little satisfies a woman when her love is great enough.

Why, then, has Lillie left you, and why does she refuse to give you an explanation?

Why does she allow you to draw the worst conclusions?

I will tell you: Lillie is in love with two men at the same time. Their different personalities and natures satisfy both sides of her character. If Schlegel had not fallen from his horse and broken his back, thereby losing all his faculties, Lillie would have remained with you and continued to be a model wife and mother. In the same way, had you been the victim of the accident, she would have clean forgotten Schlegel, and would have lived and breathed for you alone.

But fate decreed that the misfortune should be his.

Lillie had not sufficient strength to fight the first, sharp anguish. She was bewildered by the shock, and felt herself suddenly in a false position. The love on which her imagination had been feeding seemed to her at the moment the true one. She felt she was betraying you, Schlegel, and herself; and since self-sacrifice has become the law of her existence, she was prepared to renounce everything as a proof of her love.

As to you, Professor Rothe, you have acted very foolishly. You have done just what any average, conventional man would have done. Your injured vanity silenced the voice of your heart.

You had the choice of two alternatives: either Lillie was mad, or she was responsible for her actions. You were convinced that she was quite sane and was playing you false in cold blood. She wished to leave you; then let her go. What becomes of her is nothing to you; you wash your hands of her henceforth.

You write that you have only taken your two elder daughters into your confidence. How could you have found it in your heart to do this, instead of putting them off with any explanation rather than the true one!

Lillie knew you better than I supposed. She knew that behind your apparent kindness there lurked a cold and self-satisfied nature. She understood that she would be accounted a stranger and a sinner in your house the moment you discovered that she had a thought or a sentiment that was not subordinated to your will.

You have let her go, believing that she had been playing a pretty part behind your back, and that I was her confidante, and perhaps also the instigator of her wicked deeds.

Lillie has taken refuge with her children's old nurse.

How significant! Lillie, who has as many friends as either of us, knows by a subtle instinct that none of them would befriend her in her misfortune.

If you, Professor, were a large-hearted man, what would you do? You would explain to the chief doctor at the infirmary Lillie's great wish to remain near Schlegel until the end comes.

Weigh what I am saying well. Lillie is, and will always remain the same. She loves you, and such a line of conduct on your part would fill her with grateful joy. What does it matter if during the few days or weeks that she is with this poor condemned man, who can neither recognize her, nor speak, nor make the least movement, you have to put up with some inconvenience?

If Lillie had your consent to be near Schlegel, she would certainly not refuse to return to her wifely duties as soon as he was dead. It is possible that at first she might not be able to hide her grief from you; then it would be your task to help her win back her peace of mind.

I know something of Schlegel; during the last few years I have seen a good deal of him. Without being a remarkable personality, there was something about him that attracted women. They attributed to him all the qualities which belonged to the heroes of their dreams. Do you understand me? I can believe that a woman who admired strength and manliness might see in Schlegel a type of firm, inflexible manhood; while a woman attracted by tenderness might equally think him capable of the most yielding gentleness. The secret probably lay in the fact that this man, who knew so many women, possessed the rare faculty of taking each one according to her temperament.

Schlegel was a living man; but had he been a portrait, or character in a novel, Lillie would have fallen in love with him just the same, because her love was purely of the imagination.

You must do what you please. But one thing I want you to understand: if you are not going to act in the matter, I shall do so. I willingly confess that I am a selfish woman; but I am very fond of Lillie, and if you abandon her in this cruel and clumsy way, I shall have her to live with me here, and I shall do my best to console her for the loss of an ungrateful husband and a pack of stupid, indifferent children.

One word more before I finish my letter. Lillie, as far as I can recollect, is a year older than I am. Could you not—woman's specialist as you are—have found some explanation in this fact? Had Lillie been fifty-five or thirty-five, all this would never have happened. I do not care for strangers to look into my personal affairs, and although you are my cousin's husband you are practically a stranger to me. Nevertheless I may remind you that women at our time of life pass through critical moments, as I know by my daily experiences. The letter which I have written to you in a cool reasoning spirit might have been impossible a week or two ago. I should probably have reeled off pages of incoherent abuse.

Show Lillie that your pretended love was not selfishness pure and simple.

With kind greetings,

        Yours sincerely,

           ELSIE LINDTNER.

P.S.—I would rather not answer your personal attacks. I could not have acted differently and I regret nothing.

* * *

To-morrow morning I will get rid of that gardener without fail.

An extra month's wages and money for his journey—whatever is necessary—so long as he goes.

I wish to sleep in peace and to feel sure that my house is safely locked up, and I cannot sleep a wink so long as I know he comes to see Torp.

That my cook should have a man in does not shock me, but it annoys me. It makes me think of things I wish to forget.

I seem to hear them laughing and giggling downstairs.

Madness! I could not really hear anything that was going on in the basement. The birds were restless, because the night is too light to let them sleep. The sea gleams under the silver dome of the moonlit sky.

What is that? . . . Ah! Miss Jeanne going towards the forest.

Her head looks like one of those beautiful red fungi that grow among the fir-trees.

If the gardener had chosen *her*. . . . But Torp!

I should like to go wandering out into the woods and leave the house to those two creatures in the basement. But if I happened to meet Jeanne, what explanation could I give?

It would be too ridiculous for both of us to be straying about in the forest, because Torp was entertaining a sweetheart in the basement!

Doors and windows are wide open, and

they are two floors below me, and yet I seem
to smell the sour, disgusting odour of that
man.   Is it hysteria? . . .

No.   I cannot sleep, and it is four in the
morning.   The sunrise is a glorious sight
provided one is really in the mood to enjoy
it.   But at the present moment I should prefer
the blackest night. . . .

There he goes!   Sneaking away like a thief.
Not once does he look back; and yet I am
sure the hateful female is standing at the door,
waving to him and kissing her hand. . . .

But what is the matter with Jeanne?   Poor
girl, she has hidden behind a tree.   She does
not want to be seen by him; and she is quite
right, it would be paying the boor too great
an honour.

* * *

Merely to watch Richard eating was—or
rather it became—a daily torture.   He han-
dled his knife and fork with the utmost refine-
ment.   Yet I would have given anything if he
would have occasionally put his elbows on the
table, or bitten into an unpeeled apple, or

smacked his lips. . . . Imagine Richard smacking his lips!

His manners at table were invariably correct.

I shall never forget the look of tender reproach he once cast upon me when I tore open a letter with my fingers, instead of waiting until he had passed me the paper-knife. Probably it got upon his nerves in the same way that he got upon mine when he contemplated himself in the looking-glass.

A spot upon the table-cloth annoyed and distracted him. He said nothing, but all the time he eyed the mark as though it was left from a murderer's track.

His mania for tidiness often forced me, against my nature, to a counteracting negligence. I intentionally disarranged the bookshelves in the library; but he would follow me five minutes afterwards and put everything in its place again.

Yet had I really cared for him, this fussiness would have been an added charm in my eyes.

Was Richard always faithful to me? Or,

if not, did he derive any pleasure from his lapses? Naturally enough he must have had many temptations; and although I, as a mere woman, was hindered by a thousand conventional reasons, he had opportunities and reasonable excuses for taking what was offered him.

And probably he did not lose his chances; at any rate when he was away for long together on business. But I am convinced that his infidelities were a sort of indirect homage to his lawful wife, and that he did not derive much satisfaction from them. I am not afraid of being compared with other women.

After all, my good Richard may have remained absolutely true to me, thanks to his mania for having all things in order.

I am almost sorry that I never caught him in some disgraceful infidelity. Discovery, confession, scenes, sighs, and tears! Who knows but what it might have been a very good thing for us? The certainty of his unceasing attentions to me was rather tame; and he did not gain much by it in the long run, poor man.

The only time I ever remember to have felt jealous it was not a pleasant sensation, although I am sure there were no real grounds for it. It was brought about by his suggestion that we should invite Edith to go to Monaco with us. Richard went as white as a sheet when I asked him whether my society no longer sufficed for him. . . .

I cannot understand how any grown-up man can take a girl of seventeen seriously. They irritate me beyond measure.

* * *

Malthe has come back from Vienna, they tell me. I did not know he had been to Vienna. I thought all this time he had been at Copenhagen.

It is strange how this news has upset me. What does it matter where he lives?

If he were ten years younger, or I ten years older, I might have adopted him. It would not be the first time that a middle-aged woman has replaced her lap-dog in that way. Then I should have found him a suitable wife! I should have surrounded myself by a swarm of pretty girls and chosen the pick of the bunch for him. What a fascinating prospect!

* * *

I have never made a fool of myself, and I am not likely to begin now.

* * *

I begin to meet people in the forest—*my* forest. They gather flowers and break branches, and I feel as though they were robbing me. If only I could forbid people to walk in the forest and to boat on The Sound!

It is quite bad enough to have the gardener prowling about in my garden. He is all over the place. The garden seems to have shrunk since he came. And yet, in spite of myself, I often stand watching the man when he is digging. He has such muscular strength and uses it so skilfully. He puts on very humble airs in my presence, but his insolent eyes take in everything.

Torp wears herself out evolving tasty dishes for him, and in return he plays cards with her.

Jeanne avoids him. She literally picks up her skirts when she has to go past him. I like to see her do this.

* * *

This morning Jeanne and I laughed like two children. I was standing on the shore looking at the sea, and said absent-mindedly:

"It must be splendid bathing here."

Jeanne replied:

"Yes, if we had a bathing-hut."

And I, still absent-minded, murmured:

"Yes, if we had a bathing-hut."

Suddenly we went off into fits of laughter. We could not stop ourselves.

Now Jeanne has gone hunting for workmen. We will make them work by the piece, otherwise they will never finish the job. I had some experience this autumn with the youth who was paid by the day to chop wood for us.

When the hut is built I will bathe every day in the sunshine.

* * *

They are both master-carpenters, and seem to be very good friends. Jeanne and I lie in the boat and watch them, and stimulate them with beer from time to time. But it does not seem to have much effect. One has a wife and twelve children who are starving. When they have starved for a while, they take to begging. The man sings like a lark. He has spent two years in America, but he assures me it is "all tommy-rot" the way they work like steam-engines there. Consequently he soon returned to his native land.

"Denmark," he says, "is such a nice little country, and all this water and the forests make it so pretty. . . ."

Jeanne and I laugh at all this and amuse ourselves royally.

The day before yesterday neither of the men appeared. A child had died on the island, and one of them, who is also a coffin-maker, had to supply a coffin. This seemed a reasonable excuse. But when I inquired whether the coffin was finished, he replied:

"I bought one ready-made in the town . . . saved me a lot of bother, that did."

His friend and colleague had been to the town with him to help him in his choice!

The water is clear and the sands are white and firm. I am longing to try the bathing. Jeanne, who rows well, volunteered to take me out in the boat. But to bathe from the boat and near these men! I would rather wait!

* * *

Full moon. In the far distance boats go by with their white sails. They glide through the dusk like swans on a lake. The silence is so intense that I can hear when a fish rises or a bird stirs in its nest. The scent of the red roses that blossomed yesterday ascends to my window here. . . .

Joergen Malthe. . . .

When I write his name it is as though I gave him one of those caressing touches for which my fingers yearn and quiver. . . .

Yes, a dip in the sea will calm me.

I will undress in the house and wrap myself in my dressing-gown. Then I can slip through the pine-trees unseen. . . .

* * *

It was glorious, glorious! What do I want a bathing-hut for? I go into the sea straight from my own garden, and the sand is soft and firm to my feet like the pine-needles under the trees.

The sea is phosphorescent; I seemed to be dipping my arms in liquid silver. I longed to splash about and make sparkles all around me. But I was very cautious. I swam only as far as the stakes to which the fishermen fasten their nets. The moon seemed to be suspended just over my head.

I thought of Malthe.

Ah, for one night! Just one night!

* * *

Jeanne has given me warning. I asked her why she wished to leave. She only shook her head and made no answer. She was very pale; I did not like to force her to speak.

It will be very difficult to replace her. On the other hand, how can I keep her if she has made up her mind to go? Wages are no attraction to her. If I only knew what she wanted. I have not inquired where she is going.

* * *

Ah, now I understand! It is the restlessness of the senses. She wants more life than she can get on this island. She knows I see through her, and casts her eyes downward when I look at her.

* * *

J OERGEN MALTHE,
You are the only man I ever loved.
And now, by means of this letter, I am digging a fathomless pit between us. I am not the woman you thought me; and my true self you could never love.

I am like a criminal who has had recourse to every deceit to avoid confession, but whose strength gives way at last under the pressure of threats and torture, and who finds unspeakable relief in declaring his guilt.

Joergen Malthe, I have loved you for the last ten years; as long, in fact, as you have loved me. I lied to you when I denied it; but my heart has been faithful all through.

Had I remained any longer in Richard's house, I should have come to you one day and asked you to let me be your mistress. Not your wife. Do not contradict me. I am the stronger and wiser of the two.

To escape from this risk I ran away. I

fled from my love—I fled, too, from my age. I am now forty-three, you know it well, and you are only thirty-five.

By this voluntary renunciation, I hoped to escape the curse that advancing age brings to most women. Alas! This year has taught me that we can neither deceive nor escape our destiny, since we carry it in our hearts and temperaments.

Here I am, and here I shall remain, until I have grown to be quite an old woman. Therefore, it is very foolish of me to pour out this confession to you, for it cannot be otherwise than painful reading. But I shall have no peace of mind until it is done.

My life has been poor. I have consumed my own heart.

* * *

As far as I am aware, my father, a widower, was a strictly honourable man. Misfortune befell him, and his whole life was ruined in a moment. An unexpected audit of the accounts of his firm revealed a deficiency. My father had temporarily borrowed a small sum to save a friend in a pressing emergency. Henceforward he was a marked man, at home and abroad. We left the town where we lived. The retiring pension which was granted to him in spite of what had happened sufficed for our daily needs. He lived lost in his disgrace, and I was left entirely to the care of a maid-servant. From her I gathered that our troubles were in some way connected with a lack of money; and money became the idol of my life.

I sometimes buried a coin that had been given me—as a dog buries his bone. Then I lay awake all night, fearing I should not find it again in the morning.

I was sent to school. A classmate said to me one day:

"Of course, a prince will marry you, for you are the prettiest girl here."

I carried the words home to the maid, who nodded her approval.

"That's true enough," she said. "A pretty face is worth a pocketful of gold."

"Can one sell a pretty face, then?" I asked.

"Yes, child, to the highest bidder," she replied, laughing.

From that moment I entered upon the accursed cult of my person which absorbed the rest of my childhood and all my first youth. To become rich was henceforth my one and only aim in life. I believed I possessed the means of attaining my ends, and the thought of money was like a poison working in my blood.

At school I was diligent and obedient, for I soon saw it paid best in the long run. I was delighted to see that I attracted the attention of the masters and mistresses, simply because of my good looks. I took in and pondered over every word of praise that concerned my appearance. But I put on airs of modesty, and no one guessed what went on within me.

I avoided the sun lest I should get freckles. I collected rain-water for washing. I slept in gloves; and though I adored sweets, I refrained from eating them on account of my teeth. I spent hours brushing my hair.

At home there was only one looking-glass. It was in my father's room, which I seldom entered, and was hung too high for me to use. In my pocket-mirror I could only see one eye at a time. But I had so much self-control that I resisted the temptation to stop and look at my reflection in the shop windows on my way to and from school.

I was surprised when I came home one day to find that the large mirror in its gold frame had been given over to me by my father and was hanging in my room. I made myself quite ill with excitement, and the maid had to put me to bed. But later on, when the house was quiet, I got up and lit my lamp. Then I spent hours gazing at my own reflection in the glass.

Henceforth the mirror became my confidant. It procured me the one happiness of my childhood. When I was indoors I passed most of my time practising smiles, and forming my expression. I was seized with terror lest I should lose the gift that was worth "a pocketful of gold."

I avoided the wild and noisy games of other girls for fear of getting scratched. Once, however, I was playing with some of my school friends in a courtyard. We were swinging on the shafts of a cart when I fell and ran a nail into my cheek. The pain was nothing compared to the thought of a permanent mark. I was depressed for months, until one day I heard a teacher say that the mark was all but gone—a mere beauty spot.

When I sat before the looking-glass, I only thought of the future. Childhood seemed to me a long, tiresome journey that must be got through before I reached the goal of riches, which to me meant happiness.

Our house overlooked the dwelling of the chief magistrate. It was a white building in the style of a palace, the walls of which were covered in summer-time with roses and clematis, and to my eyes it was the finest and most imposing house in the world.

It was surrounded by park-like grounds with trim lawns and tall trees. An iron railing with gilded spikes divided it from the common world.

Sometimes when the gate was standing open I peeped inside. It seemed as though the house came nearer and nearer to me. I caught a glimpse in the basement of white-capped serving-maids, which seemed to me the height of elegance. It was said that the yellow curtains on the ground floor were pure silk. As to the upstairs rooms, the shutters were generally closed. These apartments had not been opened since the death of Herr von Brincken's wife. He rarely entertained.

Sometimes while I was watching the house, Herr von Brincken would come riding home accompanied by a groom. He always bowed to me, and occasionally spoke a few words. One day an idea took possession of me, with such force that I almost involuntarily exclaimed aloud. My brain reeled as I said to myself, "Some day I will marry the great man and live in that house!"

This ambition occupied my thoughts day and night. Other things seemed unreal. I discovered by accident that Herr von Brincken often visited the parents of one of my schoolmates. I took great pains to cultivate her acquaintance, and we became inseparable.

Although I was not yet confirmed, I succeeded in getting an invitation to a party at which Von Brincken was to be present. At that time I ignored the meaning of love; I had not even felt that vague, gushing admiration that girls experience at that age. But when at table this man turned his eyes upon me with a look of astonishment, I felt uncomfortable, with the kind of discomfort that follows after eating something unpleasant. Later in the the evening he came and talked to me, and I managed to draw him on until he asked whether I should like to see his garden.

A few days later he called on my father, who was rather bewildered by this honour, and asked permission to take me to the garden. He treated me like a grown-up person, and after we had inspected the lawns and borders, and looked at the ripening bunches in the grape-house, I felt myself half-way to become mistress of the place. It never occurred to me that my plans might fall through.

At the same time it began to dawn upon me that the personality of Von Brincken, or rather the difference of our ages, inspired me with a kind of disgust. In spite of his style and good appearance, he had something of the "elderly gentleman" about him. This feeling possessed me when we looked over the house. In every direction there were lofty mirrors, and for the first time in my life I saw myself reflected in full-length—and by my side an old man.

This was the beginning. A year later, after I had been confirmed, I was sent to a finishing school at Geneva at Von Brincken's expense. I had not the least doubt that he meant to marry me as soon as my education was completed.

The other girls at the school were full of spirits and enthusiastic about the beauties of nature. I was a poor automaton. Neither lakes nor mountains had any fascination for me. I simply lived in expectation of the day when the bargain would be concluded.

When two years later I returned to Denmark, our engagement, which had been concluded by letter, was made public. His first hesitating kiss made me shudder; but I compelled myself to stand before the looking-glass and receive his caresses in imagination without disturbing my artificially radiant smile.

Sometimes I noticed that he looked at me in a puzzled kind of way, but I did not pay much attention to it. The wedding-day was actually fixed when I received a letter beginning:

"MY DEAR ELSIE,

"I give you back your promise. You do not love me.

"You do not realize what love is. . . ."

This letter shattered all my hopes for the future. I could not, and would not, relinquish my chances of wealth and position. Henceforth I summoned all my will-power in order to efface the disastrous impression caused by my attitude. I assured my future husband that what he had mistaken for want of love was only the natural coyness of my youth. He was only too ready to believe me. We decided to hasten the marriage, and his delight knew no bounds.

One day I went to discuss with him some details of the marriage settlements. We had champagne at lunch, and I, being quite unused to wine, became very lively. Life appeared to me in a rosy light. Arm in arm, we went over the house together. He had ordered all the lights to be lit. At length we passed through the room that was to be our conjugal apartment. Misled, no doubt, by my unwonted animation, and perhaps a little excited himself by the wine he had taken, he forgot his usual prudent reserve, and embraced me with an ardour he had never yet shown. His features were distorted with passion, and he inspired me with repugnance. I tried to respond to his kisses, but my disgust overcame me and I nearly fainted. When I recovered, I tried to excuse myself on the ground that the champagne had been too much for me.

Von Brincken looked long and searchingly at me, and said in a sad and tired voice, which I shall never forget:

"Yes, you are right. . . . Evidently you cannot stand my champagne."

The following morning two letters were brought from his house. One was for my father, in which Von Brincken said he felt obliged to break off the engagement. He was suffering from a heart trouble, and a recent medical examination had proved to him that he would be guilty of an unpardonable wrong in marrying a young girl.

To me he wrote:

"You will understand why I give a fictitious reason to your father and to the world in general. I should be committing a moral murder were I to marry you under the circumstances. My love for you, great as it is, is not great enough to conquer the instinctive repugnance of your youth."

Once again he sent me abroad at his own expense. This time, at my own wish, I went to Paris, where I met a young artist who fell in love with me. Had I not, in the saddest way, ruled out of my life everything that might interfere with my ambitious projects, I could have returned his passion. But he was poor; and about the same time I met Richard. I cheated myself, and betrayed my first love, which might have saved me, and changed me from an automaton into a living being.

Under the eyes of the man who had stirred

my first real emotions, I proceeded to draw Richard on. My first misfortune taught me wisdom. This time I had no intention of letting all my plans be shattered.

When I look back on that time, I see that my worst sin was not so much my resolve to sell myself for money, as my aptitude for playing the contemptible comedy of pretended love for days and months and years. I, who only felt a kind of indifference for Richard, which sometimes deepened into disgust, pretended to be moved by genuine passion. Yes, I have paid dearly, very dearly, for my golden cage in the Old Market.

Richard is not to blame. He could not have suspected the truth. . . .

It is so fatally easy for a woman to simulate love. Every intelligent woman knows by infallible instinct what the man who loves her really wants in return. The woman of ardent temperament knows how to appear reserved with a lover who is not too emotional; while a cold woman can assume a passionate air when necessary.

I, Joergen, I, who for years cared for no one

185

but myself, have left Richard firmly convinced to this day that I was greedy of his caresses.

You are an honest man, and what I have been telling you will come as a shock. You will not understand it, or me.

Yet I think that you, too, must have known and possessed women without loving them. But that is not the same. If it were, my guilt would be less.

I allowed my senses to be inflamed, while my mind remained cold, and my heart contracted with disgust. I consciously profaned the sacred words of love by applying them to a man whom I chose for his money.

Meanwhile I developed into the frivolous society woman everybody took me to be. Every woman wears the mask which best suits her purpose. My mask was my smile. I did not wish others to see through me. Sometimes, during a sudden silence, I have caught the echo of my own laugh—that laugh in which you, too, delighted—and hearing it I have shuddered.

No! That is not quite true. I was a

different woman with you. A real, living creature lived and breathed behind the mask. You taught me to live. You looked into my eyes, and heard my real laughter.

How many hours we spent together, Joergen, you and I! But we did not talk much; we never came to the exchange of ideas. I hardly remember anything you ever said; although I often try to recall your words. How did we pass the happy time together?

You are the only man I ever loved.

When we first got to know each other you were five-and-twenty. So young—and I was eight years your senior. We fell in love with each other at once.

You had no idea that I cared for you.

From that moment I was a changed woman. Not better perhaps, but quite different. A thousand new feelings awoke in me; I saw, heard, and felt in an entirely new way. All humanity assumed a new aspect. I, who had hitherto been so indifferent to the weal or woe of my fellow-creatures, began to observe and to understand them. I became sympathetic. Towards women—not towards men. I do not understand the male sex, and this must be my excuse for the way in which I have so often treated men. For me there was, and is, only one man in the world: Joergen Malthe.

At first I never gave a thought to the difference in our ages. We were both young then. But you were poor. No one, least of all myself, guessed that you carried a field-marshal's baton in your knapsack. Money had not brought me happiness; but poverty still seemed to me the greatest misfortune that could befall any human being.

Then you received your first important commission, and I ventured to dream dreams for us both. I never dreamt of fame and honour; what did I care whether you carried out the restoration of the cathedral or not? The pleasure I showed in your talent I did not really feel. It was not to the man as artist, but as lover, that my heart went out.

Later, you had a brilliant future before you; one day you would make an income sufficient for us both. But you seemed so utterly indifferent to money that I was disappointed.

My dreams died out like a fire for want of fuel.

Had you proposed that I should become your mistress, no power on earth would have held me back. But you were too honourable even to cherish the thought. Besides, I let you suppose I was attached to my husband. . . .

I knew well enough that the moment you became aware of my feelings for you, you would leave no stone unturned until you could legitimately claim me as your wife. . . . Such is your nature, Joergen Malthe!

So I let happiness go by.

* * *

Two years ago Von Brincken died, leaving me a considerable share of his fortune—and a letter, written on the night of the day when we last met.

I might then have left Richard. Your constancy would have been a sufficient guarantee for my future.

A mere accident destroyed my illusions. A friend of my own age had recently married an officer much younger than herself. At the end of a year's happiness he left her; and society, far from pitying her, laughed at her plight.

This drove me to make my supreme resolve —to abandon, and flee from, the one love of my life.

Joergen, I owe you the best hours I have known: those hours in which you showed me the plans for the "White Villa."

I feel a bitter, yet unspeakable joy when I think that you yourself built the walls within which I am living in solitary confinement.

Once I longed for you with a consuming ardour.

Now, alas, I am but a pile of burnt-out ashes. The winds of heaven have dispersed my dreams.

I go on living because it is not in my nature to do away with myself. I live, and shall continue to live.

If only you knew what goes on within me, and how low I have sunk that I can write this confession!

There are thoughts that a woman can never

reveal to the man she loves—even if her own life and his were at stake. . . .

It is night. The stars are bright overhead. Joergen Malthe, why have I written all this to you? . . . What do I really want of you? . . .

*   *   *

No, no! . . . never in this world. . . .

You shall never read this letter. Never, never! What need you know more than that I love you? I love you! I love you!

I will write to you again, calmly, humbly, and tell you the simple truth: I was afraid of the future, and of the time when you would cease to love me. That is what I fled from.

I still fear the future, and the time when you will love me no more. But all my powers of resistance are shattered by this one truth: *I love.* For the first and only time in my life. Therefore I implore you to come to me; but now, at once. Do not wait a week or a month. My lime trees are fragrant with blossom. I want you, Joergen, now, while the limes are flowering. Then, what you ask of me shall be done.

If you want me for a wife, I will follow you as the women of old followed their lords and masters, in joyful submission. But if you only care to have me for a time, I will prepare the house for my desired guest.

Whatever you decide to do will be such an immense joy that I tremble lest anything should happen to hinder its fulfilment. . . .

Then let the years go by! Then let age come to me!

I shall have sown so many memories of you and happiness that I shall have henceforth a forest of glad thoughts, wherein to wander and take my rest till Death comes to claim me.

The sun is flashing on the window-panes; the sunbeams seem to be weaving threads of joy in rainbow tints.

You child! How I love you! . . .

Come to me and stay with me—or go when we have had our hour of delight.

* * *

The letter has gone. Jeanne has rowed to the town with it.

She looked searchingly at me when I gave it to her and told her to hurry so that she should not lose the evening post. Both of us had tears in our eyes.

I will never part with Jeanne. Her place is with me—and with him. I stood at the window and watched her pull away in the little white boat. She pulled so hard at the oars. If only she is strong enough to keep it up. . . . It is a long way to the town.

Never has the evening been so calm. Everything seems folded in rest and silence. There lies a majesty on sky and earth. I wandered at random in the woods and fields, and scarcely seemed to feel the ground beneath my feet. The flowers smell so sweet, and I am so deeply moved.

How can I sleep! I feel I must remain awake until my letter is in his hands.

Now it is speeding to him through the quiet night. The letter yearns towards him as I do myself.

I am young again. . . . Yes, young, young!

. . . How blue is the night! Not a single light is visible at sea.

If this were my last night on earth I would not complain. I feel my happiness drawing so near that my heart seems to open and drink in the night, as thirsty plants drink up the dew.

All that was has ceased to be. I am Elsie Bugge once more, and stand on the threshold of life in all its expanse and beauty.

* * *

He is coming. . . .

He will come by the morning train. It seems too soon.

Why did he not wait a day or two? I want time to collect myself. There is so much to do. . . .

How my hands tremble!

* * *

I carry his telegram next my heart. Now I feel quite calm. Why will Jeanne insist on my going to bed? I am not ill.

She says it is useless to arrange the flowers in the vases to-night, they will be faded by to-morrow. But can I rely on Torp's seeing that we have enough food in the house? My head is swimming. . . . The grass wants mowing, and the hedge must be cut. . . . Ah! What a fool I am! As though he would notice the lawn and the hedge! . . . . Jeanne asks, "Where will the gentleman sleep?" I cannot answer the question. I see she is getting the little room upstairs ready for him. The one that has most sun.

* * *

Has Jeanne read my thoughts? She proposes to sleep downstairs with Torp so long as I have "company."

* * *

I have begun a long letter to Richard, and that has passed the time so well. I wish he could find some dear little creature who would sweeten life for him. He is a good soul. During the last few days I seem to have started a kind of affection for him.

We will travel a great deal, Joergen and I. Hitherto I have seen nothing on my many trips abroad. Joergen must show me the world. We will visit all the places he once went to alone.

Now I understand the doubting apostle Thomas. Until my eyes behold I dare not believe.

Joergen has such a big powerful head! I sometimes feel as though I were clasping it with both my hands.

* * *

Torp suggests that to-morrow we should have the same *menu* that she prepared when the "State Councillor" entertained Prince Waldemar. Well! Provided she can get all she wants for her creations! She can amuse herself at the telegraph office as far as I am concerned. I am willing to help her; at any rate, I can stir the mayonnaise.

* * *

How stupid of me to have given Lillie my tortoiseshell combs! How can I ask to

196

have them back without seeming rude? Joergen was used to them; he will miss them at once.

I have had out all my dresses, but I cannot make up my mind what to wear. I cannot appear in the morning in a dinner dress, and a white frock—at my age! . . . After all, why not? . . . The white embroidered one . . . it fits beautifully. I have never worn it since Joergen's last visit to us in the country. It has got a little yellow from lying by, but he will never notice it.

To-night *I will* sleep—sleep like a top. Then I shall wake, take my bath, and go for a long walk. When I come home, I will sit in the garden and watch until the white boat appears in the distance.

I had to take a dose of veronal, but I managed to sleep round the clock, from 9 P.M. to 9. A.M. The gardener has gone off in the boat; and I have two hours in which to dress.

What is the matter with me? Now that my happiness is so close at hand, I feel strangely depressed.

* * *

Jeanne advises a little rouge. No! Joergen loves me just as I am. . . .

* * *

How he will laugh at me when he hears that I cried because I cannot get into the white embroidered dress nowadays! It is my own fault; I eat too much and do not take enough exercise.

I put on another white dress, but I am very disappointed, for it does not suit me nearly as well.

* * *

I see the boat. . . .

* * *

HE came by the morning train, and left the same evening. That was the day before yesterday, and I have never slept since. Neither have I thought. There is time enough before me for thought.

He went away the same evening; so at least I was spared the night.

I have burnt his letter unread. What could it tell me that I did not already know? Could it hold any torture which I have not already suffered?

Do I really suffer? Have I not really become insensible to pain? Once the cold moon was a burning sun; her own central fires consumed it. Now she is cold and dead; her light a mere reflection and a falsehood.

* * *

His first glance told me all. He cast down his eyes so that he might not hurt me again. ... And I—coward that I was—I accepted without interrupting him the tender words he spoke, and even his caress. . . .

But when our eyes met a second time we both knew that all was at an end between us.

One reads of "tears of blood." During the few hours he spent in my house I think we smiled "smiles of blood."

When we sat opposite to each other at table, we might have been sitting each side a deathbed. We only attempted to speak when Jeanne was waiting at table.

When we parted, he said:

"I feel like the worst of criminals!"

He has not committed a crime. He loved me once, now he no longer loves me. That is all.

* *

But after what has happened I cannot remain here. Everything will remind me of my hours of joyful waiting; of my hours of failure and abasement.

Where can I go to hide my shame?

* *

THE DANGEROUS AGE

Richard. . . .

*　*　*

Would that be too humiliating? Why should it be? Did I not give him my promise: "If I should ever regret my resolution," I said to him.

*　*　*

I will write to him, but first I must gather up my strength again. Jeanne goes long walks with me. We do not talk to each other, but it comforts me to find her so faithful.

*　*　*

DEAR RICHARD,

It is a long time since I wrote to you, but neither have you been quite so zealous a correspondent this summer, so it is tit for tat.

I often think of you, and wonder how you are really getting on in your solitude. Whether you have been living in the country and going up to town daily? Or if, like most of the "devoted husbands," you still only run down to the cottage for week-ends?

If I were not absolutely free from jealousy, in any form, I should envy you your new car. This neighbourhood is charming, but to explore it in a hired carriage, lined with dirty velvet, does not attract me. Now, dear friend, don't go and send off car and chauffeur post-haste to me. That would be like your good nature. But, of course, I am only joking.

Send me all the news of the town. I read the papers diligently, but there are items of interest which do not appear in the papers! Above all, tell me how things are going with Lillie. Will she soon be coming home? Do you think her conduct was much talked of outside her own circle? People chatter, but they soon forget.

Homes for nervous cases are all very well in their way; but I think our good Hermann Rothe went to extremes when he sent her to one. He is furious with me, because I told him what I thought in plain words. Naturally he did not in the least understand what I was driving at. But I think I made him see that Lillie had never been faithless to him in the physiological meaning of the word—and that is all that matters to men of his stamp.

I am convinced that Lillie would not have suffered half so much if she had really been unfaithful in the ordinary sense.

But to return to me and my affairs.

You cannot imagine what a wonderful business-woman the world has lost in me. Not only have I made both ends meet—I, who used to dread my Christmas bills—but I have so much to the good in solid coin of the realm that I could fill a dozen pairs of stockings. And I keep my accounts—think of that, Richard! Every Monday morning Torp appears with her slate and account-book, and they must balance to a farthing.

I bathe once or twice a day from my cosey little hut at the end of the garden, and in the evening I row about in my little white boat. Everything here is so neat and refined that I am sure your fastidious soul would rejoice to see it. Here I never bring in any mud on my shoes, as I used to do in the country, to your everlasting worry. And here the books are arranged tidily in proper order on the shelves. You would not be able to find a speck of dust on the furniture.

Of course the gardener from Frijsenborg, about whom I have already told you, is now courting Torp, and I am expecting an invitation to the wedding one of these next days. Otherwise he is very competent, and my vegetables are beyond criticism.

Personally, I should have liked to rear chickens, but Torp is so afflicted at the idea of poultry-fleas that she implored me not to keep fowls. Now we get them from the schoolmaster who cannot supply us with all we want.

I have an idea which will please you, Richard.

What if you paid me a short visit? Without committing either of us—you understand? Just a brief, friendly meeting to refresh our pleasant and unpleasant memories?

I am dying for somebody to speak to, and who could I ask better than yourself?

But, just to please me, come without saying a word to anyone. Nobody need know that you are on a visit to your former wife, need they? We are free to follow our own fancies, but there is no need to set people gossiping.

Who knows whether the time may not come when I may take my revenge and keep the promise I made you the last evening we spent together? When two people have lived together as long as we have, separation is a mere figure of speech. People do not separate after twenty-two years of married life, even if each goes a different road for a time.

But why talk of the future. The present

concerns us more nearly, and interests me far more.

Come, then, dear friend, and I will give you such a welcome that you will not regret the journey.

* * *

Joergen Malthe paid me a flying visit last week. Business brought him into the neighbourhood, and he called unexpectedly and spent an hour with me.

I must say he has altered, and not for the better.

I hope he will not wear himself out prematurely with all his work.

If you should see him, do not say I mentioned his visit. It was rather painful. He was shy, and I, too, was nervous. One cannot spend a whole year alone on an island without feeling bewildered by the sudden apparition of a fellow-creature. . . . .

Tell your chauffeur to get the car ready. Should you find the neighbourhood very fascinating, you could always telegraph to him to bring it at once.

If the manufactory, or any other plans, prevent your coming, send me a few lines. Till we meet,

Your ELSIE,

who perhaps after all is not suited to a hermit's life.

* * *

So he has dared! . . .

So all his passion, and his grief at parting, were purely a part that he played! . . . Who knows? Perhaps he was really glad to get rid of me. . . .

Ah, but this scorn and contempt! . . .

Elsie Lindtner, do you realise that in the same year, the same month, you have offered yourself to two men in succession and both have declined the honour? Luckily there is no one else to whom you can abase yourself.

One of these days, depend upon it, Richard will eat his heart out with regret. But then it will be too late, my dear man, too late!

That he should have dared to replace me by a mere chit of nineteen!

The whole town must be laughing at him. And I can do nothing. . . .

But I am done for. Nothing is left to me, but to efface myself as soon as possible. I cannot endure the thought of being pitied by anyone, least of all by Richard.

How badly I have played my cards! I who thought myself so clever!

Good heavens! I understand the women who throw vitriol in the face of a rival. Unhappily I am too refined for such reprisals.

But if I had her here—whoever she may be —I would crush her with a look she could never forget.

* * *

Jeanne has agreed to go with me.

Nothing remains but to write my letter— and depart!

* * *

D EAREST RICHARD,
How your letter amused me, and
how delighted I am to hear your in-
teresting intelligence. You could not have
given me better news. In future I am re-
lieved of all need of sympathetic anxiety
about you, and henceforth I can enjoy my freedom without a qualm, and dispose of life just
as I please.

Every good wish, dear friend! We must
hope that this young person will make you
very happy; but, you know, young girls have
their whims and fancies. Fortunately, you
are not only a good-looking man in the prime
of life, but also an uncommonly good match
for any woman. The young girls of the present day are seldom blind to such advantages,
and you will find her devotion very lasting, I
have no doubt.

Who can she be? I have not the least idea.
But I admire your discretion—you have not
changed in that respect. In any case, be pre-

pared, Richard, she will turn the house upside down and your work will be cut out for you to get it straight again.

I am sure she bikes; she will probably drop her cigarette ashes into your best Venetian glasses; she is certain to hate goloshes and long skirts, and will enjoy rearranging the furniture. Well, she will be able to have fine times in your spacious, well-ordered establishment!

I hope at any rate that you will be able to keep her so far within bounds that she will not venture to chaff you about "number one." Do not let her think that my taste predominates in the style and decorations of the house. . . .

Dear friend, already I see you pushing the perambulator! Do you remember the ludicrous incident connected with the fat merchant Bang, who married late in life and was always called "gran'pa" by his youthful progeny? Of course, that will not happen in your case—you are a year or two younger than Bang, so your future family will more probably treat you like a playfellow.

You see, I am quite carried away by my surprise and delight.

If it were the proper thing, I should immensely like to be at the wedding; but I know you would not allow such a breach of all the conventions.

Where are you going for the honeymoon? You might bring her to see me here occasionally, in the depths of the country, so long as nobody knew.

One of my first thoughts was: how does she dress? Does she know how to do her hair? Because, you know, most of the girls in our particular set have the most weird notions as regards hair-dressing and frocks.

However, I can rely on the sureness of your taste, and if your wedding trip takes you to Paris, she will see excellent models to copy.

Now I understand why your letters got fewer and farther between. How long has the affair been on hand? Did it begin early in the summer? Or did you start it in the train between Hœrlsholm and Helsingœr, on your way to and from the factory? I only ask —you need not really trouble to answer.

I can see from your letter that you felt some embarrassment, and blushed when you wrote it. Every word reveals your state of mind; as though you were obliged to give some account of yourself to me, or were afraid I should take your news amiss. I have already drunk to your happiness all by myself in a glass of champagne.

You can tell your young lady, if you like.

Under the circumstances you had better not accept the invitation I gave you in my last letter; although I would give much to see your good, kind face, rejuvenated, as it doubtless is, by this new happiness. But it would not be wise. You know it is harder to catch and to keep a young girl than a whole sackful of those lively, hopping little creatures which are my horror.

Besides, a new idea has occurred to me, and I can hardly find patience to wait for its realisation.

Guess, Richard! . . . I intend to take a trip round the world. I have already written to Cook's offices, and am eagerly awaiting information as to tickets, fares, etc. I shall not go alone. I have not courage enough for that. I will take Jeanne with me. If I cannot manage it out of my income, I shall break into my capital, even if I have to live on a pittance hereafter.

No—do not make any more of your generous offers of help. You must not give any more money now to "women." Remember that, Richard!

The White Villa will be shut up during my absence; it cannot take to itself wings, nor eat its head off during my absence. Probably in future I shall spend my time between this place and various big towns abroad, so that I shall only be here in summer.

At the same time as this letter, I am sending a wedding present for your new bride. Girls are always crazy about jewellery. I have no further use for a diadem of brilliants; but you need not tell her where it comes from. You will recognise it. It was your first overwhelming gift, and on our wedding day I was so taken up with my new splendour that I never heard a word of the pastor's sermon. They said it was most eloquent.

I hope you will have the tact to remove the too numerous portraits of myself which adorn your walls. Sell them for the benefit of struggling artists; in that way, they will serve some good purpose, and I shall not run the risk of being disfigured by my successor.

If I should come across any pretty china, or fine embroidery, in Japan, I shall not forget your passion for collecting.

Let me know the actual date of the wedding, you can always communicate through my banker. But the announcement will suffice. Do not write. Henceforth you must devote yourself entirely to your rôle of young husband.

You quite forgot to answer my questions about Lillie, and I conclude from your silence that all is well with her.

Give her my love, and accept my affectionate greetings.

ELSIE LINDTNER.

P.S.—As yet I cannot grapple with the problem of my future appellation. I do not feel inclined to return to my maiden name.

"Elizabeth Bugge" makes me think of an overgrown grave in a churchyard.

Well, you will be neither the first nor the last man with several wives scattered about the globe. The world may be a small place, but it is large enough to hold two "Mrs. Lindtners" without any chance of their running across each other.